This book is dedicated to anyone who's ever had to fight for their own happiness.
Especially me.

Dying for Rain
Synopsis

What could be worse than knowing the exact day the world is going to end?

Waking up to find out that it didn't.

The post–April 23 world is a lawless, senseless, ruthless place, but it's not loveless. At least, not for Rain and Wes.

But when the government begins holding daily televised executions as a demonstration of their power, that love is put to the ultimate test.

Will Rain sacrifice one life to save the others?

Or sacrifice the others to save *the one*?

May 5
Rain

IT'S AMAZING HOW YOUR whole life can change in an instant. How forces beyond your control can just reach out and rip entire chunks of your life away from you—the best chunks, the biggest chunks—without so much as a *please* or a *thank you.* And those forces always wait until your guard is down. They want to hear you exhale, to sigh in quiet contentment, before they strike.

I was in my tree house after sundown, exhaling a calming stream of smoke from one of my daddy's cigarettes, when three shotgun blasts made me an orphan.

I was creeping down the highway on the back of Wes's motorcycle, relieved that we'd survived April 23 and excited about what we might find outside of Franklin Springs, when an eighteen-wheeler exploded and almost killed my best friend, Quint.

I was wrapped in the safety of a dark, abandoned bookstore, sleeping peacefully after making love to Wes, when he ripped *himself* out of my life without so much as a goodbye.

And I'm in the safety of Wes's arms now, in the living room of my childhood home, surrounded by a newly polished hardwood floor and freshly painted walls, when I feel myself exhale again.

Watch my fear flutter to the floor like a silk robe.

Smile as hope and peace and gratitude tickle my flushed skin and whisper promises in my ear.

Wes wraps my thighs around his waist and kisses that smile away—feverishly, impatiently. As if he has more love to give me than time.

I sigh into his mouth, and three knocks on the door immediately signal my mistake. I let my guard down again, and now, the forces have come to take the only good thing I have left.

My eyes slam open, and Wes grabs my face.

"Hey, it's okay. You're gonna be okay."

"What's gonna be okay? What's happening, Wes?"

Bang, bang, bang!

"Georgia State PD. Open up!"

I shriek and cover my mouth with my hands. My stupid, sighing mouth.

"We have the premises surrounded! Open up!"

"Oh my God!" I search Wes's face for answers, search the room for a place to hide.

"They're not here for you." He shushes me, cupping my cheek in his warm, rough hand. "You did nothing wrong, okay? Just promise me you'll stay here. You're safe here."

"What's happening, Wes?" My voice goes shrill as the banging gets louder.

"It's open!" Wes yells, holding my stare as the door behind me—the brand-new country-blue door that he installed while he was away—flies open.

"That's him," a voice I've known—a voice I've *trusted*—my entire life snarls from the doorway. "That's the man who procured the antibiotics."

I spin around as my mouth falls open, shock and betrayal slicing me from back to front as I turn. "Mrs. Renshaw! What are you doing?"

I block Wes with my body as my eyes dart from Carter's mom to the massive police officer standing next to her. Rage and hurt and a desperate kind of fear surge through me, making my movements jerky and forcing words out of my mouth.

"It was me!" I scream. "Take me! I gave Quint the antibiotics! Not Wes!"

The cop flashes Mrs. Renshaw a questioning look as Wes calmly walks around my outstretched arms and kneels before me in the middle of my living room. My fingers weave through his hair, pulling it away from his face as tears blur my vision.

"No …" I whisper.

"It was me. I saved Quinton Jones's life," Wes announces without taking his eyes off me. "And even if it wasn't, you can't execute her …"

I shake my head down at him, pleading with him to do something.

And he does. He presses a single kiss to my belly and smiles up at me, a mixture of pride and heartbreak carved into his beautiful features.

"She's pregnant."

Those words bounce off my brain, heard but rejected, as the cop yanks Wes off the ground by his arm.

"You have the right to remain silent. Anything you say can and will be used against you—"

"No!" I scream, lunging for Wes. I grab his blue Hawaiian shirt with both hands as the meathead standing behind him clasps a pair of metal handcuffs around his innocent wrists.

He might as well be tightening a noose around his neck.

"Stop it! You're killing him!" I shout.

"You will be given an audience with the governor within seventy-two hours—at which point, you may defend yourself against the charges being brought against you."

I glance up at Wes's face, expecting to find panic mirroring my own, but for once, his pale mossy eyes aren't analyzing or angry or guarded or cold. They're just sad.

Sad and so, so sorry.

"Eyewitness testimony and evidence collected at the scene of the crime will be taken into consideration," the officer drones on, ignoring me as he continues his speech, but Mrs. Renshaw gives me her full attention.

"Rainbow, let go!" she hisses, taking a step toward me. "This man is a danger to everyone in the community. One day, you'll see—"

"You're killing him!" I scream again, this time directing my rage at the woman standing next to the officer. I've never wanted to hit anyone so badly in my life, but my hands won't let go of Wes.

I can't let go of Wes.

Instead, I wrap my arms around his shoulders, bury my face in his chest, and scream directly into the thick flesh and thin cotton separating me from his heart.

How many beats does it have left?

How many would it have had if he'd never met me?

Wes presses his lips to the top of my head as my lungs finally run out of air, and it breaks me all the way.

Because I know this kiss. I know all of his kisses.

Wes is trying to comfort me.

But who's going to comfort him?

"Ramirez? You need backup?" a gruff voice calls from my open doorway.

"Yeah. Looks like we got a stage five clinger."

"Ma'am," the second officer snaps, "I'm gonna need you to let go of the suspect and step aside."

I hear the order, but I don't look up or even acknowledge it. It doesn't matter anyway. I couldn't let go of Wesson Patrick Parker if I tried.

And I've been trying for weeks.

"Ma'am, this is your final warning. I will not ask you again. Let go of the suspect and put your hands on your head."

"Rainbow! Let go!" Mrs. Renshaw yells.

"Let go, baby," Wes whispers into my hair. "I love you so fucking much. Just do what they say, okay?"

But I can't. His shirt is so soft. His chest, so warm. His heart, so steady and strong where it pounds against my cheek. I clutch his shoulders tighter and stifle a sob as I press up onto my toes and kiss his worried mouth. Wes's bottom lip pulls free from his teeth just before it collides with mine. Then, he stills, holding the moment along with his breath.

He doesn't kiss me like our time is running out.

He kisses me like it's already up.

And he's right. Because before I have a chance to whisper that I love him too—before I can say goodbye to the man who taught me how to live—fifty thousand volts of electricity say it for me, seizing my muscles and bringing me to my knees.

Wes

THE FEELING OF RAIN'S body seizing against mine, the helplessness of watching her tumble to the floor at my feet—my handcuffed arms unable to catch her convulsing body—it destroys whatever's left of me.

As the officer drags me toward the front door, I feel my soul, my heart, my fucking will to live disappearing with every step I take. They don't belong to me anymore. Honestly, they never did. They belong to the little black-haired rag doll twitching on the floor back there.

By the time that asshole shoves me down the front steps, the crushing pressure in my chest is reduced to a hollow ache—just phantom pains from my amputated heart. By the time we get to his pig mobile, I hardly remember having feelings at all. And by the time he shoves me inside and slams the door, I've gone completely … fucking … numb.

I was never meant to get the girl. To have the happily ever after. That's not how my world works, and this shit right here is proof. Rain has shelter, a means of self-defense, and money to get supplies. There's nothing left for me to do. My girl—and my kid, if my suspicions are right—are going to have as good a life as anyone could hope for post–April 23.

And me?

In a few days, I'll be fucking fertilizer, and I won't have to feel this shit at all.

Rain

"SWEETHEART, I DID YOU a favor. I did all of us a favor. One day, you'll see.

"Are you *really* expecting, dear? How long has it been since you got your cycle?

"A baby! Oh my goodness. What a blessing!

"Don't you worry. Mama Renshaw's gonna help you every step of the way. And Carter—oh, he's gonna be such a good daddy.

"I'm gonna be a grandma!

"Sit up, child. I got you some water."

When I don't comply, Mrs. Renshaw cuts the happy rambling and switches into high school administrator mode. "Rainbow, *sit up*," she hisses, snapping her fingers at me.

"Don't be so dramatic. I know you think you loved that man, but in time, you'll realize that you only got attached to him because you'd just lost your folks. He was a monster, dear. You saw what he did to my sweet Carter. We're all safer with him gone."

"You're the monster." The words aren't much louder than a whisper as they leak out of my parted lips and dribble down my cheek onto the hardwood floor.

"Excuse me?"

I swallow, tasting blood and feeling pulses of pain radiating from one side of my tongue. I must have bitten it during the tasing.

"*You're* the monster," I repeat, clearing my throat.

I don't open my eyes. Don't lift my head. I'm in the same sloppy fetal position I ended up in after the volts hit me, and I don't plan on moving. Ever.

A new pain, deep and dull, throbs in my lower back, right where Wes tucked his gun into my waistband before the cops showed up.

I squeeze my eyes shut tighter and silently thank him for this last gift.

"Rainbow, I know you're upset, but when you're feeling better—"

"I will never feel better."

And as soon as you leave, I'm gonna put a bullet in my head to match the one you just gave Wes.

"I remember feeling that way too, when I was expecting Sophie. I thought I'd never feel better. But after the first trimester, you'll get your spark back."

I hear metal scraping wood just a few feet away from my head and realize that Mrs. Renshaw must be picking up the key that I dropped. The one Wes placed in my palm right after we got here. A few minutes—that's all it took for this woman to rip my future away from me. A few minutes is all it ever takes.

"Is that my front door? It is, isn't it? Goodness gracious! If that ain't a sign from God, I don't know what is. It's like he's sayin', *Welcome home, Agnes!*" Mrs. Renshaw's voice cracks, and she sniffles back a sob.

"We're gon' be all right, baby girl." Her weathered hand pats my exposed shoulder. "The Lord is my shepherd; I shall not want."

"Get out," I manage to rasp even though my lungs feel like they're going to collapse under the weight of my despair.

"You're right. I should go. You probably want some alone time. I'll be back to check on you a little later, dear. Be sure to drink your water."

Just as I hear her footsteps retreat toward the door, they stop a moment later and return to my side twice as fast as they left. "Oh, I almost forgot …"

The back of my tank top lifts, and the revolver Wes tucked into my waistband is jerked free. I hear the *click, spin, clack* of Mrs. Renshaw checking the barrel for bullets on her way out the door.

Then, I pull my knees to my chest, wrap my arms around them, and sob myself unconscious.

No dreams come to distract me from my thoughts of death. No visions of my parents or Wes arrive to soothe me. When I wake up—minutes later, hours maybe—I am empty. I am alone.

I am dead.

I just have to muster the strength to get up and make it official.

I push myself onto my hands and knees and crawl over to the stairs. The third one creaks under my weight. So does the fifth. And the sixth. This is the only home I've ever known, and it feels like it's saying goodbye with every squeaking floorboard and groaning joist.

For the first time since I heard those shotgun blasts, I'm not afraid to go into my parents' room. Nothing can hurt me anymore.

Not for long, at least.

I turn the corner into the master bedroom, but this time, I don't find the faceless body of my mother lying in a pool of blood with the shades drawn shut. I find an empty wooden bedframe, illuminated by the afternoon sun. The curtains are wide open. The mattress and bedding, long gone. All traces of what happened here … erased. It almost makes me feel bad for what I'm about to do. For leaving another bloody mess in the house that Wes spent so much time cleaning up.

Maybe I should do it in the backyard, I think.

Maybe it doesn't fucking matter anymore.

I flip the light switch in my parents' walk-in closet out of habit and am surprised when the overhead bulb actually comes on.

The second I see their clothes, the smell of them hits me like a sledgehammer.

Stale cigarettes and hazelnut coffee.

I want to wrap my arms around my mother's hanging dresses and make them hug me back. I want to sway with them and stroke their sleeves against my cheek. But what would be the point?

To make myself feel better?

Or to make myself feel worse?

Instead, I reach in between them and find a vintage briefcase I know will be there, hanging from a nail on the wall behind Mama's church clothes.

I set the brown tweed case on the floor, spin the numbers on the little dial to 503—my birthday—and pop the dull brass tabs open with a click. Inside is foam lining, molded around a small black handgun. Daddy used to let me shoot cans off a tree stump with this one, back before he turned scary. He said this one didn't have much "kick."

I hold my breath and slide the magazine out, just like he showed me. It's empty.

But not for long.

Crawling out of the closet and into the master bathroom, I sit cross-legged on the floor in front of the vanity. I open the cabinet doors and dig all the way to the back, knocking over bottles and boxes and brushes until I find it—the jewelry box where Mama hides Daddy's bullets.

Hid.

My heart pounds against my ribs as I pull the whitewashed wooden container out, both because of what it holds and because of what I find hiding behind it.

A hot-pink cardboard box.

With a picture of a manicured hand holding a pregnancy test on the front.

I set the jewelry box down beside me and reach for the pink rectangle with wide eyes and shaking fingers. The plastic sticks inside rattle when I pick it up. Opening the box, I notice that one of the tests is missing. I know Mama was pregnant for a while back when I was a kid, but she lost that baby after a bad fight with Daddy. She told me it was God's will.

I knew better.

I check the expiration date. Then, I blink and check it again.

These tests aren't twelve years old. They're current.

"Oh, Mama. What did you do?" I whisper, tears blurring the date on the side of the box.

Whatever that test told her, it went with her to the grave.

Like mother, like daughter, I think, sliding a stick out of the box.

I flip it over and read the instructions, noticing that it says this brand can detect a pregnancy seven to ten days after conception.

God. Wes might actually be right.

His words echo in my hollow soul as I wander over to the toilet.

"She's pregnant," he'd announced, cupping my belly, his eyes shining with sorrow and pride.

I couldn't process those words at the time. I was too busy watching my entire world crumble at my feet. Too busy dismissing it as just a clever tactic to keep me from taking his place. But as I wait for the results—loading bullet after bullet into the magazine of my daddy's gun, even though I only need one, just to give my shaking fingers something to do—I think about what he said again.

And realize that I never got my birth control shot in April.

I never even thought about it. The world was about to end, and my boyfriend—*ex*-boyfriend—had just left for Tennessee.

But then I met Wes.

And the world didn't end.

It was handcuffed and ripped out of my arms instead.

I slide the clip back into the handle and take a deep breath. The gun is heavier when it's fully loaded, both with the weight of the bullets and the weight of what they could do. But when I pick up the plastic stick lying on the counter, when I read those eight letters glowing on its digital screen, it feels even heavier than the gun.

PREGNANT.

I lift my head to look at my reflection in the mirror above the sink, but I don't even recognize the girl staring back. Short black hair. An inch of blonde roots. Pistol in one hand. Positive pregnancy test in the other. And a dark, desperate madness in her sunken eyes that I haven't seen since the day my daddy put a shotgun in his mouth.

I drop both the test and the gun into the sink and take a step backward with a gasp.

You're pregnant, the girl in the mirror whispers to me.

"Honey, we're home," a voice calls from downstairs.

Rain

MRS. RENSHAW'S CHEERY VOICE from downstairs spurs me into action. My jeans are too tight to stick the gun in my pocket, so I tuck it into the back of my waistband, replacing the one Mrs. Renshaw stole. I shove everything else back inside the cabinets and shut them as quietly as I can. Then, I turn off the lights and dart across the hallway to my bedroom. I find what I'm looking for on the floor by the closet, right where I left it—Carter's oversize Twenty One Pilots hoodie. I pull it on and sigh in relief when I see how well it hides the pistol.

"Rainbooow!" This time, it's Sophie's voice I hear.

Guilt seizes my chest when I think about what she might have found up here if …

I push those thoughts out of my mind and try to clear the emotion from my throat. "Hey, Soph!" I croak out, testing my fake smile. I go to tell her that I'll be down in a minute, but before the words can form in my mouth, I hear the clomping of eager footsteps flying up the stairs.

"Rainbow!"

I barely have time to spread my arms before I find myself being tackle-hugged by my favorite ten-year-old. I expect her to begin chattering away about how she got here, but instead, she buries her face in my sweatshirt and bursts into tears.

"Hey … what's going on?" I smooth my hand over her long braids and pull her tighter.

"I'm just … I'm just so happy." She sniffles, wiping her wet eyes on the soft black cotton. "I didn't think we were ever gonna get outta that place. I didn't like it there. There were no beds and we had to shower in the rain and the big kids were so mean. And then your friend beat up Carter and took you away, and I was so scared."

Sophie lifts her little face and gives me a grin so big that I notice she's missing at least two teeth. "But Mama knew what to do. She called the police, and they found you! And they put that bad man in jail!"

Her hug lit a candle of joy in my heart, but her words blew it right back out.

"When Mama came back, she said God was so proud of her that he blessed us with a new house *and* a new baby!" Her little overwhelmed eyes fill with tears again, and all I can do is hug her tighter so that I won't have to look at them anymore.

Instead, I have to look at her brother as his six-foot-three-inch frame fills my bedroom doorway. His shirt is splattered with blood. His lips and one eyebrow are split open. His left eye is swollen shut. His nose is puffy and slightly crooked, and his usual cocky swagger has been replaced by a dark thundercloud of anger.

His one open eye narrows at the sight of me. Mine widen at the sight of him.

"Is it true, Rainbow?" Sophie squeals. "Are you really gonna have a baby?"

I hold Carter's stare, feeling the same question hanging in the air between us. Then, I sigh and tell her the truth, "Yes, sweetie, I am."

Carter's gaze drops to his sister's back as he takes in those four little words.

"Are we really gonna live here? With you? Forever?"

"Of course we are, shrimp," Carter grumbles through his mangled mouth, cutting me a warning glance. "Look." His eyes dart to something over my shoulder. "Rain's already got your bed ready."

Sophie and I both turn, and I'm shocked to discover that he's right. The last time I saw it, my bed had a shotgun blast right through the middle, but now it's covered in a pristine unicorn-mermaid-cat comforter. Wes must have gone next door and swapped out my mattress and bedding for Sophie's. He mentioned that he was able to salvage some stuff from the front half of their house.

I didn't realize he'd meant a whole bed.

With every step I take toward it, I feel closer to him. Closer and yet so much further away. I lift one knee and crawl onto the soft surface, my hand sliding across the place where a giant hole used to be. I lie with my back to my uninvited guests and pull the spare pillow to my chest. It doesn't even smell like smoke.

It smells like fabric softener.

He even washed it.

Closing my eyes, I surrender to my tears. The first ones I've let fall since he was ripped from my arms.

Wes might be the one who was taken away in handcuffs, but I'm the one facing a life sentence. This house is my prison. This baby and that little girl behind me—they're my wardens. As long as they're alive, I'll be here, suffering, because I can't take the easy way out if it means causing them pain.

"Rainbow? Are you crying?"

"Nah, she's just snorin'. Growing a baby makes you real tired. Why don't you go tell Mama that your bed's here? She'll be so happy."

"Okay!"

I hear Sophie stomp back down the stairs just before the door closes with a quiet snick.

The hair on the back of my neck stands up as the floorboards creak under Carter's heavy feet. I expect to feel the bed sag under his weight, but when it doesn't, I turn and find him pacing back and forth across my matted carpet.

His eyebrows are furrowed, his swollen lips move as if he's mumbling to himself, and his long fingers are tugging on his overgrown black curls.

I've never seen him so distraught. It makes me nervous.

"How did you guys get here?" I ask, hoping to take his mind off of whatever has him acting this way.

"My mom went back to our house, got my dad's truck out of the garage, and drove to the mall to pick us up." He shrugs. "Told us she was takin' us home."

"How did your dad get to the truck with his broken leg?"

"I pushed him in that rolly chair you gave him."

"And y'all didn't see any Bonys?"

Carter turns and glares at me with his one good eye. "Can we not do this?"

"What?"

"Pretend like everything's fucking fine."

I sigh and roll onto my back, feeling my dad's gun dig into my spine. "Fine with me."

Carter doesn't say anything. He just keeps pacing, and I just keep staring at his battered face.

"I'm sorry," I finally mutter, not knowing where else to begin.

"It's not your fault," he replies without taking his eyes off the floor. "Birth control is only, like, ninety-nine percent effective."

Wait. What?

"I just … I'm not ready to be a dad."

Oh my God. That's what he's upset about? He thinks this baby is his?

The thought seems absurd, but when I think about it, it's probably only been about two months since Carter and I were together. Two months that feel like two lifetimes. That was back before his family packed up and left me in Franklin Springs without a second glance. Back when my parents were still alive.

Back when my birth control shot was still effective.

"You're not gonna be a dad." I sigh, trying not to roll my eyes.

"I'm not?" Carter stops pacing and looks over at me again.

I shake my head, bracing for the brunt of his anger when he realizes that the man who mangled his face is the same one who knocked me up. But instead, Carter's split lips spread into a wide grin as he bounds over to give me a hug.

"Holy shit, girl! You had me worried there for a sec. I'm so glad we're on the same page! Listen, I got you. I'll take you to the clinic, I'll pay for the procedure, whatever you need. Just do me a favor and tell my mom you had a miscarriage, okay?"

I'm stunned speechless as Carter squeezes me a second time.

"Hey, boy!" Mr. Renshaw's gruff voice calls from the bottom of the stairs. "Your mother says the highway's clear all the way into town now. I'm goin' on a Burger Palace run. You wanna come with?"

"Hell yeah!" Carter fixes his one open eye on me and grins.

That's when I notice that he's missing about as many teeth as his sister. Wes really did a number on him.

Makes me love him even more.

"Dude, I haven't had a King Burger in weeks! You want one? Wait. Duh. Of course you want one. Pregnant chicks are always hungry. I'll get you two!"

Carter bounds out of my room, leaving the door wide open as I curl even tighter around the pillow in my arms.

"Will you boys get a King Burger combo for me, a Big Kid box for Sophie, and—oh, what the heck? Grab us some milkshakes, too! We're celebratin'!"

"Mama, I found a DVD player! Can I watch a movie?"

"Of course, princess! You can watch whatever you want! And while we wait for the boys to get back, Mama's gonna go take a nice hot bath. Praise be to God!"

I get up and close my bedroom door, locking it as quietly as possible before sagging against it and sliding to the floor. I stare at Sophie's bed, standing in the spot where mine used to be, and realize that I don't even have a home anymore.

This is *their* house now.

I'm just the ghost that haunts it.

Wes

THE RIDE DOWNTOWN HAS taken hours so far, thanks to all the roads that still haven't been cleared. At one point, the cops pulled over and called for an industrial-sized snow plow to come and escort us the rest of the way in, which has given them even more time to talk about which steroids to use now that they're legal and what the going rate for pussy is on the open market.

I checked out of their conversation somewhere near the Mall of Georgia and have been staring out the window ever since. It's a game I used to play on the school bus to take my mind off whatever the fuck had happened at my foster home the night before or whatever the fuck was gonna happen when I got to school that morning. I watch for road signs, streetlights, telephone poles—shit like that—and give each one a different sound in my mind. Telephone poles are the bass line. *Bum, bum, bum, bum.* Nice and steady. When a Stop sign comes by, it's a hi-hat. *Ching!* Road signs might be hand claps or dog barks or fucking jingle bells—whatever. It doesn't matter. What matters is that by the time I get to whatever shithole I'm going to, I've already forgotten about the one I just came from.

But when the street signs morph into double razor-wire fencing and the telephone poles are replaced by watchtowers, the symphony in my head fades away. Now, all I can hear is the steady beat of blood rushing into my extremities. *Fulton County Jail* the words above the front entrance announce. Hell, even the building looks like it could stab you. Beige concrete with hallways jutting out in all directions like a twelve-story high asterisk. I'm sure the inside is even less inviting, but I wouldn't know.

I've never been to jail before.

Not because I didn't deserve it. Just because I never got caught.

We approach the main entrance, but instead of pulling in and getting cleared by a guard, we drive right past the front gates. The guard stand is empty, and the gates are wide open.

Then, I remember what that French bitch, the director of the World Health Alliance, said on the April 24 announcement.

"In an effort to protect the law of natural selection going forward and to ensure that our population never again faces extinction due to our irresponsible allocation of resources to the weakest, most dependent members of society, all social services and subsidies are to be discontinued. Life support measures are to be discontinued. Government-provided emergency services are to be discontinued, and all incarcerated members of society will be released."

The jails are empty.

"Where are you taking me?"

"And if you pay her in hydro … ooooh-wee! She'll do this thing with her tongue where—"

I debate raising my voice and asking again, but then I realize that it doesn't fucking matter.

Nothing matters anymore.

I turn and look back out the window. As I follow the razor wire with my eyes, a sizzle beat begins to float into my head. Like the sound of an electric chair being warmed up.

A few turns later, just as the shiny gold dome of the capitol building comes into view in the distance, we encounter something I haven't seen in weeks. Maybe months.

Traffic.

Cars are parked and double-parked along every main street and side street as far as I can see. Some aren't even facing the right direction, and some are pulled right up onto the sidewalks—probably so their drivers can solicit the services of the naked ladies Officer Friendly and Deputy Dickface were talking about. That, or they're buying drugs from the pop-up bong stands a few feet away. They definitely aren't down here to window shop. Every store I've seen since we passed the jail has either been looted or burned.

Downtown Atlanta feels like Times Square on New Year's Eve—only instead of confetti, it's raining ashes from a nearby car fire; instead of fireworks, you hear gunshots; and instead of wearing stupid plastic sunglasses and carrying inflatable noisemakers, the women aren't wearing anything, and the men are carrying machine guns.

The cops flip on their siren to try to get through, but nobody pays them any attention. Nobody, except for the working girls who turn and twiddle their fingers at their best customers.

"Damn it!" The cop driving slams his palms against the steering wheel. "We're gonna have to call Hawthorne again."

"I'm on it." The cop in the passenger seat snatches the CB radio off the dash. "Hey, Sheryl. It's Ramirez. Can you send Hawthorne to help bring us in? We're on the corner of Northside Drive and MLK."

"Again? Don't y'all know not to go that way?"

"It's blocked every damn which-a-way, Sheryl. Just send Hawthorne. I ain't walkin' this suspect ten blocks down MLK."

"Okay, fine. You don't have to be so salty about it."

"And tell him to hurry up!" Ramirez slams the CB back in its cradle.

Gunshots ring out in the distance, but like the siren, nobody on the street seems to notice.

"They really need to get us a damn helicopter. This is bullshit," Ramirez huffs, crossing his arms and shifting in his seat. His knee is bouncing so fast it's making the car shake, and I realize that he's jonesing for something.

"Hey, I'mma go get a blow job real quick. You want anything?"

"Come on, man. Hawthorne's gonna be here in less than ten minutes."

"It'll only take me five," Ramirez sneers. As soon as he pushes his door open, white noise explodes into the car—a deafening mixture of hip-hop, techno beats, gunshots, car horns, dogs howling, women screaming, and alarm systems going off. But when Ramirez slams his door shut, it goes almost completely silent again.

Must be the bulletproofing.

"Fuckin' dumbass," Officer Friendly mutters under his breath.

Opening the center console, he takes out a flask and unscrews the cap with a flick of his hairy-knuckled thumb. As he brings it to his lips, his eyes, shadowed by a Neanderthal-like brow bone, cut to mine in the rearview mirror. He takes a swig. Then, he turns to face me.

"Want some?" he asks, holding the flask out and giving it a little shake.

When I shrug, he chuckles, his meaty face contorting into something even uglier.

"Oh, right. You're a little tied up, huh?"

Suddenly, something slams into the windshield, causing Officer Asshole to drop his flask and scramble for his gun. I look up to find a guy crouching on the hood of the car, peering in at us through the eyeholes of a King Burger mask. Skeleton features have been smeared onto it with neon-orange paint, matching the bone-like stripes spray-painted on his black hooded sweatshirt.

The car begins to bounce violently as another Bony, and then another, leap onto the hood, the roof, the trunk. The zombified King Burger twists his head from side to side, like a raptor studying its prey, before he takes a gun out of his hoodie pocket and presses the barrel to the glass.

I duck just before the concussion of bullets and splintering glass rings in my ears.

Ka-boom!

Ka-boom!

Ka-boom!

Ka—

Thud.

The car stops shaking.

The bullets stop flying.

And the sounds of downtown Atlanta fill the air again as Ramirez hops back inside and slams the door.

"Goddamn, I hate those motherfuckers!"

I sit back up to find King Burger slumped against the bulletproof glass, his lifeless eyes halfway open as blood trickles down his mask, filling every crack in the shattered windshield.

"That's the third car we've fucked up this week! The chief is gonna be so pissed."

"If he'd buy that damn helicopter, this wouldn't keep happening!"

Officer Friendly turns to look out his side window. "'Bout fucking time."

I follow his gaze and notice blue flashing lights reflecting in the broken shop windows on MLK Jr. Drive as a behemoth of a SWAT tank comes barreling into view. It's two lanes wide, and it has a metal blade on the front that's at least a foot thick. People on the street scatter like rats, jumping into their parked cars and trying to get the fuck out of the way before they get smashed.

Officer Friendly flips on the PA system and grabs the microphone. "Thanks a lot, good buddy," he announces through the loudspeakers as the tank grinds past. Then, he throws the car in drive and turns left onto MLK once the intersection is clear, leaning all the way to the left to see around the shattered windshield and the dead body on the hood.

"Why don't *we* ever get to drive the Scorpion?" Ramirez whines.

"Because we weren't military, remember?"

"Hawthorne should at least let me shoot the cannon some time."

Officer Friendly drives a few blocks and turns left onto Central Avenue where a huge crowd of people is gathered in a park.

"Oh shit! We got a dead man walkin'!"

The cop car slows to a crawl, and I do the stupidest thing I could possibly do.

I turn and look out my window.

The left and right sides of the park are lined with spectators, standing behind metal barricades and kept at bay by at least a dozen riot cops holding machine guns. On the far side of the plaza, a woman in a burlap jumpsuit is standing with her back to me. A row of freshly planted saplings stretches out to her left, and Governor Fuckface and a TV crew are standing to her right.

My guts twist.

No. No, no, no, no, no.

Keep driving!

But they don't. They pull to a complete stop and watch as the woman's head suddenly snaps backward. Her body jerks, her knees buckle, and the earth swallows her whole.

Stomach acid claws its way up my throat, but I swallow it down and squeeze my eyes shut. I tell myself that it's not a bad way to go. It's instant. Clean. There are way worse ways to die.

Cancer is worse. Disembowelment, terrible. I could be burned at the stake or locked in an iron maiden. I could be—

Ramirez lets out a low whistle. "There goes Nora. What a waste of a good pair of tits."

"Didn't she bite you?"

"Fuck yeah, she did. Had to get a tetanus shot and everything. But you know I like 'em feisty."

As Officer Friendly chuckles and shifts into drive, I take a deep breath and one last look at the place where Nora used to be.

And that's when I see him.

The executioner.

Black mask.

Black police uniform.

Black fucking soul.

And when his head follows our car as it pulls into the police station across the street, I know he sees me too.

Wes

"GODDAMN IT, RIGGINS! THAT'S the third car this week!"

"It wasn't my fault, sir! We got stuck in traffic, and the Bonys swarmed us!"

"I told him not to take Northside Drive, sir."

"Shut up, Ramirez! Y'all are lucky you still have jobs, you know that?"

I drum my fingers against the molded plastic armrest of the 1970s-era chair I'm handcuffed to as Ramirez, Officer Friendly—who I guess is named Riggins—and their police chief argue about the dead Bony they rode in with. The lobby of the Fulton County Police Department feels like a DMV waiting room from 1975—other than the flat screen TV glowing on the wall. Reporter Michelle Ling is interviewing

Governor Fuckface in Plaza Park right down the street. The sound is off—thank God. But even without being able to hear his pompous-ass voice, that jowly grin and puffed-out belly speak volumes. He's as proud of his "duty to protect the laws of natural selection" as Michelle Ling is nauseated by the sight of him. I can see it on her face. Either she polished off a fifth of gin before this interview or this man makes her sick to her stomach.

Maybe both.

Probably both.

Just then, an officer breezes in through a side hallway with the swagger of a seasoned drag queen. He seems vaguely familiar, but it might just be because he looks like RuPaul with a little more meat on his bones and a lot less style.

"Miss me, bitches?" He sweeps a hand across the nearly empty room and then grimaces when his eyes land on the chief. "Sorry, Your Majesty." He curtsies.

"Elliott," the police chief snaps. "Deal with *that* until Hoyt and MacArthur get back." He points directly at me and then goes back to ripping Riggins and Ramirez a pair of new assholes.

"Ugh. Processing?"

The chief cuts him a warning glance, and Elliott pouts pretty hard before coming over. But as he crosses the dingy tiled floor, his face morphs from annoyed to impressed.

"Well, helloooo, sailor. I'm loving the Hawaiian print." He swirls a long index finger at me. "Very '90s Leo."

I lift an eyebrow, waiting for him to get to the point, and he lifts one right back as if he's waiting for me to respond.

Finally, he huffs, "You don't know who I am?"

Now, both of my eyebrows are raised. I shake my head a fraction of an inch, and his face falls.

"Really? Okay, maybe this will jog your memory." He backs up about ten feet and walks toward me again, this time with a blank expression on his face and an invisible person on the crook of his arm.

Considering that I just saw a sneak preview of my own death a few minutes ago, I'm not really in the mood for fucking charades, but I decide to throw the guy a bone. Maybe because he's the only person around here who isn't acting like a 'roided-out douche bag.

"The bailiff? From the executions?" I tilt my head toward the glowing screen in the corner of the room.

"Ding-ding-ding!" He beams, clapping his hands with every *ding*. "You probably didn't recognize me because I'm sooo butch on TV." The sound of footsteps entering the lobby makes him snap his head toward the back hallway. "Aren't I, Mac?"

"Aren't you what?" the gruff, middle-aged guy walking in mutters back. He doesn't even look at us. His gaze is fixed on the cubicle he's walking over to, and his shoulders are rounded from carrying the weight of the world on them.

"Aren't I so butch on TV? Our new suspect—" Elliott turns to me and asks, "What's your name, handsome?"

"Wesson Parker," I deadpan.

"Ooh, Wesson. Like the gun? I like that. Very *Dirty Harry*."

Elliott turns back to the guy who is now sitting with his back to us at a computer screen. "Wesson here didn't even recognize me! Can you believe that?"

"Nope," he mutters. Then, he pulls the trash can out from under his desk and blows a snot rocket into it.

"That's MacArthur. He's a sourpuss, but he loves me. Don't you, Mac?"

"Hmmph," the old guy grumbles, pecking at his yellowed keyboard with two stiff index fingers.

Just then a dude about as wide as the hallway he's walking through comes lumbering into the station lobby.

"Oh, thank God! Hoyt! Hoyt, c'mere, sweetie!" Elliott waves at him like a damsel in distress.

About thirty slow-motion strides later, the slack-jawed, sleepy-eyed, shaggy-haired officer makes it over to us. He reminds me of a sheepdog, both in his appearance and general IQ, but sheepdogs probably smell better.

"Hoyt, the chief told me *to tell you* to process this fine young man as soon as you got back." Elliott tosses me a wink that goes completely unnoticed by Officer Hoyt.

He simply nods and produces a key ring from his front pocket. Unlocking the metal bracelet attached to the armrest, he gestures for me to stand and secures my wrists behind my back again. Hoyt doesn't make eye contact once. He simply takes me by the arm and shuffles me over to a cubicle next to MacArthur's.

After he takes my fingerprints, name, and basic info—with as few words uttered as possible—Officer Hoyt uses a key card to escort me through a security door and into a dimly lit hallway. He stops at a metal cabinet, digs around inside for a minute, and pulls out a cup, a toothbrush, an orange jumpsuit, and a plastic bottle marked *De-Licer.*

"Sorry, man," he mumbles, his head hanging even lower than before. "Gotta hose ya down."

"Better you than the bailiff," I deadpan.

Officer Hoyt opens the floor-to-ceiling cabinet door a little wider until it blocks the small black video camera attached to the ceiling behind it. Then, for the first time since we met, he lifts his head and looks me dead in the eye. The pity and remorse I see there hit me right in the fucking gut. He doesn't look at me like I'm a suspect or a convict or "the accused." He looks at me like I'm a man who just found out that he only has a few days left to live.

"For what it's worth," he whispers, blinking his red-rimmed eyes, "I really am sorry."

I nod and press my lips together to keep my chin from wobbling like a little bitch.

I'm gonna fucking die here, I think as he escorts me to the showers.

"Dead man walkin'."

May 6
Rain

I COULDN'T SLEEP, SO I came out to the front porch to get some fresh air and escape Jimbo's snoring. He and Mrs. Renshaw dragged their king-size mattress over from next door and flopped it across my parents' queen-size bedframe last night, and Carter tossed his mattress on the floor in our junk room. Now the whole house smells like smoke.

It smells like their house.

Because it *is* their house now.

The morning fog has settled in Old Man Crocker's field across the street. It looks like a fallen cloud being pierced by orange and pink lasers as the sun rises behind the pine trees.

And that's when I realize … I'm outside.

I haven't been able to come outside without having a panic attack in weeks, but here I am. *Not* panicking.

Probably because there's nothing left to fear.

I step off the porch and walk down the stairs where Wes and I sat just yesterday afternoon.

My feet carry me past my daddy's rusted old truck—the one that Wes siphoned all the gas out of the day we met—and they don't stop.

They take me down to the end of the driveway, where about six envelopes are scattered on the gravel. I pick them up one by one.

Franklin Springs Electric.

Franklin Springs Natural Gas.

Franklin Springs Water and Sewer.

First Bank of Georgia.

They're all addressed to Mr. and Mrs. Phillip Williams.

I run my fingertips over their names, but I feel nothing. Just the slick surface of the clear plastic film covering them. Then, I fold the stack of unpaid bills in half and tuck it into my hoodie pocket.

I pick my fallen mailbox up next. The wooden post is broken off at the ground level, so I shove what's left of it into the soft Georgia clay next to the driveway. It only sticks about two feet above the ground now, but I don't care.

I don't care about anything anymore.

"Welcome to *Fuck*lin Springs!" the sign across the street greets me as I pass, not reading my mood.

I haven't walked down the highway into town by myself in months. Not since the crime rate skyrocketed, the roads got clogged with wrecks and cars that had run out of gas, and the local cops stopped showing up for work. After that, I mostly kept to the trail that snaked through the woods. But I'm not worried about the bad guys getting me now.

In fact, I hope they do.

The birds seem to be singing louder than ever as I walk past the torched and dilapidated farmhouses that used to belong to my neighbors. Maybe it's because I haven't heard one in weeks. They're damn-near deafening now.

I have to walk in the middle of the street because all the wreckage has been shoved to the sides of the highway. Thanks to Quint. When the world was busy going insane on April 23, he grabbed his little brother and his daddy's bulldozer and figured out a way to get the hell out of town.

A lot of good that did. Quint almost died in a bulldozer explosion, and now Wes is going to be executed for saving his life. I wish we'd never followed them out of town.

The second I think it, I want to take it back. If we hadn't followed them, if we hadn't been there, Quint would have died. I picture him and Lamar, all alone with that evil bitch, Q, and her crazy gang of runaways, and I shake my head. She's gonna eat them alive.

Maybe I can convince Carter to take the truck back to the mall and get them, too.

As the glowing Burger Palace billboard rises over the trees in the distance, King Burger appears to be galloping toward me with his French fry staff held high. In the place where it used to say, *Apocasize it!* above a photo of the King Burger combo meal, it now says, *Natural selection is the king's way!* with a digital slideshow of all their combo selections below.

The sign disgusts me so much it makes my stomach turn. A wave of nausea brings me to a halt, and I barely manage to pull my hair away from my face before I buckle at the waist and puke on the side of the road. Once the last heave leaves me, I prop my forearm on the wrecked minivan next to me and drop my forehead onto it. As the hurricane in my stomach dies down, I open my eyes and glance at the woman reflected in the tinted glass.

"*You're pregnant*," she whispers to me again.

"I know that," I snap back.

Pushing away from the burgundy van, I continue walking, but this time with a destination in mind.

The closer I get to Burger Palace, the louder the sounds of civilization become. Cars stretch down the street in the oncoming lane, waiting to pull in to the parking lot. Toddlers tantrum and mothers yell and grown men curse at each other from their driver's seats as they jockey for position and cut each other off in line.

In front of Burger Palace, walking up and down the side of the highway, are street vendors pandering to the captive audience.

"AK-47 for sale! Perfect condition! Only fired once!"

"Spare change? I gotta feed my babies, y'all! Spare change?"

"Hydro! Oxy! Adderall! Viagra! No prescription necessary!"

"You fellas like to party? Fifty bucks each. Seventy-five if it's at the same time."

I flip my hood up and stick to the opposite side of the road. Cars and trucks and four-wheelers and even a few tractors pass me as they pull out of Burger Palace, but nobody stops.

They can tell I've got nothing left to offer.

I walk past the hollowed-out shell of the old library and inhale the scent of scorched books.

I walk past *Shart*well Park, careful not to step on any used hypodermic needles.

And finally, once the sun has risen above the tree line and the sweat has begun to trickle down my back, I see it.

Fuck*abee Foods.*

The nausea returns full force as I look across the nearly empty parking lot and remember what happened here just a few weeks ago. The three thugs who died right outside those sliding glass doors—one from overdosing on the pills Wes had given him to pay our way inside, the other two from a spray of bullets.

Fired by me.

Even though the few businesses that haven't been looted or torched are up and running again, I knew better than to expect Huckabee Foods to be one of them. The redneck mafia of Franklin Springs would rather burn this place to the ground than relinquish control. Which is why I'm not at all surprised to see a new red-bandana-wearing, facial-tattoo-sporting, machine-gun-carrying asshole sitting in a lawn chair outside.

The sight of those guys used to make me want to turn and run in the opposite direction, but that was back when I still cared about what happened to me.

Now all I care about is getting what I need and getting the hell out of here.

I pull the gun out of the back of my jeans and approach the front door with it pointed toward the ground.

Captain No-Neck looks up from his cell phone and does a double take when he sees me.

"Daaaamn, girl. That sassy walk you got is makin' my dick hard. Come on over here and give me some sugar." He spreads his legs and rubs the crotch of his pants. "I'll make it worth ya while."

I feel my heart begin to race as I stop about fifty feet away. From here, I can see that the glass in the sliding door has been replaced with a blue tarp, and there's still a red stain on the cement in front of it.

"Here's how this is gonna work," I say, trying to keep my voice as steady as possible. "You're gonna go inside and get me all the prenatal vitamins you can find, plus some canned fruits and veggies and soup with meat in it. It's gotta have meat. When you come back out, there'll be a hundred-dollar bill tucked underneath the windshield wiper of that blue Toyota." I tip my head in the direction of the car closest to him. "You take the money and leave the groceries, and nobody gets hurt."

The guard snorts through his nose before erupting into full-blown laughter. "Homegirl, the only thing that's gonna get hurt around here is yo' pussy."

"That's what the last guy said who was sittin' in that chair."

His face hardens. "What the fuck did you say?"

"He was a big fella, too, just like you. In fact, I think that's his gun you're holdin'. I know 'cause I used it to shoot your two friends over there." My eyes cut to the red stain on the cement next to him.

His jaw snaps shut, and his eyes narrow in hatred. "You tellin' me you killed Skeeter and Lawn Boy?" His voice sounds like a dangerous combination of rage and grief, so I soften my tone.

"Only 'cause they fired first. Like I said, I don't wanna hurt anybody. But you got what I need in there, and I ain't leavin' without it."

The tattooed testosterone machine's nostrils flare as he considers my proposition. Then, he stands up and swings the Uzi toward me, biceps flexing as he squeezes the handle in anger. I close my eyes and hold my breath, but the *br-r-r-r-ap* never comes.

"Two hundred," he finally says with a frustrated growl. "For Skeeter and Lawn Boy."

I nod solemnly. "Two hundred."

When the behemoth turns and passes through the sliding tarp door, I exhale in relief and dig a wad of cash out of my back pocket with a shaking hand. It's everything I had hidden in my sock drawer. Figured I'd better keep it on me now that my house has been overrun by Renshaws.

With knocking knees, I walk over to the blue Toyota and tuck all my twenties under the passenger windshield wiper. Then, I retreat to the F-150 a few parking spaces away.

Visions of an ambush flood my mind while I wait. I picture the guard running out with five, ten, fifteen thugs on his heels, all of them blasting the parking lot with semiautomatic weapons until the dumb girl in the baggy hoodie is just another red stain on the cement.

Maybe that's the real reason I came here.

Maybe I *want* them to kill me.

But they don't. What feels like hours later, the tarp door slides open again, revealing guard number two holding four plastic grocery bags and looking none too pleased about it.

He makes murderous eye contact with me as he lumbers toward the blue sedan. Then, he drops the bags on the hood and snatches the cash out from under the wiper blade.

Counting it twice, the leathery redneck spits on the ground in my direction. Then, he turns and walks back to his station.

I wait until he's back in his lawn chair and as far away from me as he's going to get before I approach the car. He watches me walk with a predatory stare but doesn't make a move as I inspect the bags. It's all here—the vitamins, the soup, the fruits and veggies. This time, I can't keep my tears at bay as an overwhelming mixture of pride and disbelief swells in my chest.

"Thank you," I say, my voice cracking as I give the ogre a small, sincere smile.

"Fuck you," he replies, dropping his eyes back down to the phone in his lap.

Wes

THREE HUNDRED FIFTY-FOUR.

No matter how many times I count the gray cinder blocks lining my six-by-six cell, it always comes out to three hundred and fifty-fucking-four.

It's so small I can't even lie down on the cot without bending my knees, which is exactly what I'm doing as I stare at the ceiling with my pillow pressed against my ears, trying to block out the sobs of the guy in the holding cell next to me.

Sad bastard kept me up all night. I'd felt bad for him at first, but now, I wish somebody would come put him out of his misery. I don't know how much more of this shit I can take.

His guttural wails finally die down—*thank God*—but before I can roll over and try to get some shut-eye, the fucker decides he wants to chat.

"Hey, neighbor? You doing okay?" He sniffles, blowing his nose on God knows what.

Ugh. Do we really have to do this?

"Yep," I deadpan.

"I'm sorryyyyy." His voice breaks on the last syllable, and the tears start up again. "I'm trying to be quiet … I really am."

Jesus fucking Christ.

"It's cool," I mutter without an ounce of sincerity. I'm not exactly long on compassion right about now.

"I'm Doug." He sniffle-snorts like a rusty trumpet.

"Wes."

"Hi, Wes. What are you in for?"

Oh my God.

I roll my eyes. This guy sounds like a pocket-protector-wearing Trekkie with a comb-over and a degree in Norse mythology. He must have heard that line in a prison movie on Netflix.

"Antibiotics." Accepting that I'm never going to sleep again, I sit up and stretch my legs out in front of me. It's weird to see them wrapped in an orange jumpsuit. I wore the same Hawaiian shirt and pair of jeans ever since the fires broke out in Charleston. All I got out of town with were the clothes on my back and my buddy's dirt bike.

Now, I don't even have those.

"Antibiotics? Wow. That's all it takes, huh?"

"Guess so. What about you?" I ask, suddenly curious about what this cubicle-dweller could have possibly done to land himself here.

"I … I stole an incubator from the hospital for m-m-my premature son." He starts weeping again, and I immediately regret asking the fucking question. "My wife and I, we …"

"Hey, man. You don't have to—" I interrupt, trying to spare myself a fucking sob story, but Doug just keeps on going.

"We'd been trying to have a baby for years. We did everything—spent our life savings on medical procedures—but nothing worked." He clears his throat, trying to pull his shit together, and continues, "When the nightmares began, we were almost relieved. There was no point in trying if the world was going to end, you know? But as soon as we gave up, that's when it happened. My wife finally got pregnant … but the baby wasn't due until *June*."

Fuck. I shake my head, staring at the floor now instead of the ceiling. I think I liked it better when he was crying.

"My wife, she … she lost it. The nightmares, the hormones, the fact that she was growing a child she'd never get to hold—it took its toll. You know how the announcement said that the April 23 hoax was designed to increase the global stress levels until the weakest members of society self-destructed?"

"Yeah," I rasp.

"My wife was weak, Wes."

Was. Past tense.

"Doug … fuck, man … I'm—"

"She … she made herself go into labor. I don't know how she did it, but on April 20, I found her in a bathtub full of blood … holding our s-s-son."

The sobbing starts again, and I can't help but think about Rain. I think about the night I found her on the verge of death with a stomach full of pills. I think about the hours I spent with my fingers down her throat, saving her life. I think about her panic attacks and trauma triggers and the days she spent holed up in an abandoned mall because she was too scared to go outside without me. Then, I think about the baby she might be growing, and I realize that my girl and Doug's girl have a lot in fucking common.

Maybe too much.

"I'm sorry for yer loss," a third voice mumbles, pulling me away from my spiraling thoughts.

I look up to find Officer Hoyt standing outside our cells, holding a pair of ankle shackles and staring at the floor.

"Oh God. Is it time? I … I'm not ready!"

"Not yet," Officer Hoyt mutters to my neighbor. "Governor Steele has a sentencin' to do first."

Then, he flashes me a remorseful, sidelong glance.

"Mr. Parker, I'm afraid I have to escort you to the courtroom now. Please stand with your back against the bars."

Regret and panic shoot through my veins as Hoyt gestures for me to step forward.

"Stick your foot out through the bars, please."

I do as he said and feel a metal shackle clamp down around my ankle.

"Other foot now."

"Doug," I ask, suddenly needing to know how his story ends, "if you're in here, does that mean you saved your son's life?"

Hoyt finishes shackling my legs and instructs me to stick my hands out through the bars next.

"Yes." Doug sniffles as cold steel greets my wrists. "I think he's going to pull through. My sister has him now."

My cell door opens with a deafening squeak. As Hoyt leads me out by the elbow, I turn and glance at the man imprisoned beside me. He's an older guy—maybe forty? Forty-five? His hair is thinning, and his skin is so pale I wouldn't be surprised if the only light it saw was the glow of a computer screen. He's wearing a blue button-up shirt with jeans and athletic shoes that have obviously *never* been used for athletics. He lifts his head as I pass and meets my sympathetic frown with one of his own, despair oozing out of his unshaven pores.

He looks like something I've always wanted. Something I'll never get the chance to become.

He looks like a dad.

A damn good one.

Rain

TWENTY-FOUR HUNDRED.

I take the last bottle of prenatal vitamins out of the plastic Huckabee Foods bag and place it on the floor of my tree house next to the others.

Twenty-seven hundred.

I don't know how far along I am, but I'm guessing that two thousand seven hundred prenatal vitamins is more than enough to get me through.

I slump back in my beanbag chair.

If Wes had seen me, he would have been so proud.

And so pissed.

I smile, remembering how mad he got the last two times we went to *Fuckabee* Foods. He told me I was "impulsive" and had a "death wish."

Yeah, and he got shot in the shoulder because of it.

My face falls.

And I let the wound get infected.

I pull my hoodie sleeves over my hands and press my fists against my mouth.

And then he almost died in Carter's house fire because I rushed back in to get his medicine and he couldn't find me.

I close my eyes and inhale through my nose. My sweatshirt smells like the vanilla candles I used to burn in my bedroom. The ones he brought with him when he came back to get me from the mall.

It's all I have left of him now. These memories … this smell …

My stomach churns again, reminding me of one more thing he left me with. Something that, unlike a scent or a memory, will only grow bigger and stronger with time. Something that, God willing, I'll be able to keep forever and ever.

My gaze drifts over to the spot across the yard where the red dirt is piled up in two neat rows as long and wide as coffins. The spot where the people who made *me* now lie. I stare at it for what feels like hours, waiting for the panic to come—the grief I've been running away from ever since that night—but it doesn't.

All I feel right now is the still, silent, soul-crushing weight of acceptance.

I climb down the ladder and trudge across my backyard, picking my feet up high as I wade through the knee-high grass. The sun is directly overhead now, but it's shady under the oak tree where Mama and Daddy are buried. I realize once I get over to them that I don't know which is which. Wes buried them while I was passed out on the bathroom floor. The mound on the left looks a little bigger, so I decide that that one must be Daddy. I turn away from him and face the mound on the right.

"Hi, Mama."

A squirrel peeks out at me from behind a branch.

"I don't know if you know this, but … I'm gonna be a mama too."

A bird chirps in response.

"I probably won't be as good of one as you"—I ball up my sleeves in my fists—"but I'm gonna try."

The wind chimes I made in art class tinkle and twirl.

"I got vitamins today … prenatal ones. And fruits and veggies, too." I beam through my sudden tears. "Aren't you proud of me?"

A gentle breeze whips around me, ruffling my hair like one of Daddy's noogies.

Silent tears stream down my face, but I don't fall apart. I wipe my runny nose on the sleeve of my sweatshirt and tell my parents what I came over here to say, "I love you guys … I'm so sorry they did this to you."

The moment the words leave my heart, I feel a little bit lighter. Not because the weight of my grief has lessened—I don't think it ever will—but because I'm carrying it differently now. It used to feel like a ball and chain around my ankle, but now, I've picked it up and put it on like a backpack.

I feel a little bit stronger.

A little bit more capable.

And for the first time in days, I feel really, really *hungry*.

I don't want to leave them. I don't want to go back into that house with those people and all that stuff that isn't mine, but I have to start thinking about more than just myself. Everyone I've lost has a chance to live on through this baby. Their blood flows in its tiny veins. If I can bring it into the world safe and sound, I might even get to see them again.

The baby might have my mother's mischievous smile or my father's button nose. I might be able to gaze into Wes's pale green eyes again or run my fingers through his soft brown hair.

My heart skips a beat as I turn and head for the back door.

Water. I need water. And a can opener. And a spoon.

I jiggle the handle and sigh when I realize that it's locked. *Of course.* I knock on my own damn door and wait for someone to let me in.

Seconds later, I hear the click-clack of the deadbolt. The door swings open, revealing one squeaky-clean Carter Renshaw wearing nothing but a pair of loose athletic shorts, as shiny and black as his sopping wet curls and bruised eye.

"There you are." He tries to smile but then hisses as his fat lip splits open again. He dabs the cut with his finger and steps aside to let me in. "We were looking for you everywhere."

"Really?" I deadpan as I walk past him into my dining room. *Their* dining room.

The sight of Carter with his shirt off used to instantly turn me on.

Now, it just pisses me off.

"Where were you? My mom made pancakes."

My mouth waters instantly as I pass through the doorway into the kitchen. The aromas of pancakes and sausage and coffee fill the air. My eyes land on Mrs. Renshaw, drying her hands on a dishtowel as Sophie wipes down the counter.

"Well, good mornin', sunshine." She beams, turning to face me.

I'm shocked at how different she looks. She must have found a wig in the wreckage of their old house because her hair is suddenly sleek and shoulder-length, like she used to wear it, and I swear she even has on mascara. Her dress is ironed. Sophie's, too. And they're both wearing probably every piece of jewelry they own.

"Rainbow!" Sophie cheers, bouncing over to give me a hug. Her plastic bracelets rattle with every step.

I mechanically wrap my arms around the girl and glare at her mother over her head. It's the first time I've seen Mrs. Renshaw since Wes was taken yesterday, but my urge to stab a utensil in her eye is put on hold when she grins and lifts a plate in my direction. My stomach growls out loud when I see what's on it.

"How did you—"

"When life gives you a box of Hungry Jack, runnin' water, and a freezer full of thawed deer sausage, you make breakfast! And lucky for us, y'all had pancake syrup!"

Sophie releases me and skips back over to the counter to get me a fork and knife from the drawer.

"Thank you," I say to Sophie instead of her mother, accepting the cutlery as Mrs. Renshaw's sparkling eyes land on her son.

"Carter, why don't you keep Rainbow company while she eats?"

The intention I see in them makes my stomach turn and my jaw clench but not enough to keep me from devouring this food.

I walk back into the dining room with Carter on my heels and sit down without acknowledging his presence. Not that he even notices. He plops down across from me and begins rambling on about everybody he saw at Burger Palace last night.

"Yo, you remember JJ, right? From the football team? That motherfucker is *swole* now. He was standing right out front, sellin' steroids and workout videos! Can you believe that shit? And I swear to God, I saw Courtney Lampros blowin' somebody between two parked cars. I'd know that fake red hair anywhere."

Yeah, I bet you would.

I swallow my last bite without even tasting it and hear someone begin talking even louder than Carter up in the living room.

"Good morning. This is Michelle Ling, reporting live from inside the Fulton County Courthouse."

My fork clatters onto my plate as I dart up the five or six stairs to the living room, where Mr. Renshaw is sprawled out on the couch with his poorly splinted leg propped up on the coffee table, messing with the remote control. He points it at the TV, mashing buttons with his knobby thumb in vain.

"Gotdamn it! I was right in the middle of watchin' *Hillbilly Handfishin'*! Now I ain't gonna know what happens!"

"We are hours away from today's public execution—"

"Then why in the hell are you interruptin' my show *now*?" Mr. Renshaw barks, chucking the now-worthless remote onto the coffee table.

"But we are going to start bringing you even more exclusive, behind-the-scenes footage from the capitol as Governor Steele works tirelessly to enforce the new law"—her face is sallow and lifeless, and she sounds as if she's reading from a script, no doubt prepared by the governor himself—"beginning with the first-ever televised sentencing."

Michelle Ling sweeps an apathetic hand out beside her and pushes open a massive wooden door. It swings wide, revealing a courtroom as big as a grocery store and as empty as church on Monday.

There's no jury.

No plaintiffs or defendants.

No witnesses waiting to be called forward.

The pews are all vacant, except for a few uniformed officers.

And there, standing next to the raised wooden judge's podium, is a tall, slender, bald man I recognize instantly as the bailiff from the executions.

Upon seeing the camera, he adjusts his uniform, lifts both hands as if he's about to conduct a symphony, and shouts, "All rise! The honorable Governor Beauregard Steele is presiding."

The two officers in the front row stand as Governor Steele breezes in through the doorway behind the bailiff. He's wearing a black judge's robe, but he left it wide open in the front to accommodate his sizable belly, and the sleeves are about three inches too short.

"Be seated."

The chair behind the podium squeaks loudly as Governor Steele sits and taps the tiny microphone in front of him,

"Ladies and gentlemen, I declauh that the Georgia State Superiuh Court is now in session. I hereby call to order the case of the People Versus …" Governor Steele shuffles a few papers around on the podium until the bailiff comes over and whispers something in his ear. "Wesson Patrick Parkuh!"

He slams his gavel down, and I feel the blow directly in my own chest.

No. No, no, no.

"Bailiff!" He swings his gavel in the direction of the man on his right with the enthusiasm of a game show host. "Bring out the accused!"

I'm no longer in my body. I'm not even in my living room. I'm in the back row of that courtroom, clutching the smooth wooden bench in front of me so hard that my knuckles turn white as the bailiff pushes through the door behind him and reenters the room, dragging Wes by the elbow.

My Wes.

The camera zooms in on his beautiful face, and thanks to the power of HDTV, I can count every black eyelash as he stares at the floor, every stubborn strand of hair that refuses to stay tucked behind his ear, and every worried crease in his lips as he chews on the corner of his mouth. He's right there. Larger than life. So close I can touch him.

So, I do.

I step toward the TV as Mrs. Renshaw and Sophie and Carter come running up the stairs. Wes's eyes stare back at me the moment my fingertips graze his cheek, but they're not happy to see me.

They're downright hateful.

"Rainbow! Get away from there!" Mrs. Renshaw snaps. "Jimbo, don't just sit there! Turn that godforsaken thing off!"

"I tried, Agnes! They're broadcastin' it on every damn channel!"

"Well, try harder!"

"Your Honor." The camera cuts away from Wes and over to the judge's stand, where one of the police officers in the front row is now addressing the governor.

I yank my hand back and stumble away from the screen.

"The accused has been charged with violating the one and only true law, the law of natural selection, by procuring and administering life-saving antibiotics to a mortally wounded citizen. The evidence will show that an open bottle of Keflex was found at the scene of the crime with the accused's fingerprints on it, and the accused was identified on sight by an eyewitness. I motion to find the accused guilty as charged."

Governor Steele leans back in his chair and folds his hands across his stomach. "Very good then. Very good. Does the, uh, defense have anything to say?" He turns a beady eye on the second officer in the front row, who stands at attention and violently shakes his head.

"Jimbo! Turn! It! Off!"

"I'm tryin', woman!"

"Very well then." Governor Steele nods at the mute officer in approval, and his chair squeaks loudly as he leans forward and breathes into the microphone. "Mistuh Parkuh …"

The bailiff drags Wes over to the judge's stand, but Wes doesn't hurry. He crosses the courtroom on long, lazy legs, taking his time as the bailiff jerks on his elbow. With his hands cuffed and ankles shackled, he still manages to make that orange jumpsuit look cool as he stands in a carefree pose before the governor. Wes, the Ice King. He only acts that way when he feels threatened. It makes me want to reach into the TV and hug him from behind. Wrap my arms around his waist and rest my cheek on his back, like I used to when we would ride through the woods on his dirt bike.

Back when we thought the world was going to end.

Right now, I wish it had.

"Mistuh Parkuh, in the face of such irrefutable evidence, I hereby find you guilty of defying the one true law, the law of natural selection. You shall be sentenced to death by public exe—"

The screen goes black as Mrs. Renshaw yanks the plug out of the wall behind the TV stand.

"There!" she huffs, smiling at her son's busted face. "Justice is served. Now, let's all get back to enjoying this beautiful—"

I lunge. One look at Mrs. Renshaw's painted red lips, spread in a wide smile, and I see red everywhere. I let out a primal, soul-deep scream as we both tumble to the floor, synthetic hair and synthetic pearls flying as I wrap my hands around the neck of the woman who single-handedly took everything from me that April 23 hadn't already claimed.

"Rainbow! What the fuck?"

"Stop it, Rainbow. You're hurting her!"

"Gotdamn it, child! Get offa her!"

Mrs. Renshaw's eyes bulge out of her face, but I only squeeze harder, unable to stop myself even if I wanted to. Her arms flail, slapping, clawing, and tugging at my arms and wrists, but I'm too far gone. All I hear is her voice over and over in my head.

"Justice is served!"

"Justice is served!"

"Justice is served!"

I jerk her neck after every declaration. Just as her arms go limp and her eyes roll back in her head, I feel a pair of hands as big as dinner plates wrap around my waist and lift me off of her lifeless body.

"What the fuck is wrong with you?" Carter shouts as he jerks my arms behind my back, tangling them in a knot so tight I feel like the slightest move might break my shoulders.

Mrs. Renshaw comes to with a gasp, blinking and panting as she rubs the red marks around her neck.

Sophie picks up her mother's lost wig and kneels by her side, gently helping her sit up so she can place the nightmarish thing back on her head.

"What in the Sam Hill has gotten into you, child?" Mr. Renshaw asks as he hobbles over to help his wife stand.

Smoothing her dress over her wide hips, Mrs. Renshaw adjusts her wig and levels me with a lethal stare. It's the same look she saved for the really bad kids back when she was an administrator at our high school.

"Carter, Sophia … tie her up."

Wes

KEEP YOUR POSTURE LOOSE. Stop clenching your fucking jaw. Look bored. More bored.

"Mistuh Parkuh, in the face of such irrefutable evidence, I hereby find you guilty of defying the one true law, the law of natural selection. In the great state of Georgia, those who commit crimes against naychuh shall be *returned* to naychuh; therefore, I sentence you to death by public execution. This court is adjourned!" Governor Fuckface bangs his gavel and points it at the news crew standing in the back of the courtroom. "Back to you, missy!"

I glance over my shoulder just in time to see the reporter roll her eyes in disgust before turning to face the camera.

"This is Michelle Ling, reporting live from the Fulton County Courthouse. This sentencing was brought to you by Buck's Hardware … because the *buck* stops here. We'll be broadcasting live from Plaza Park this afternoon for another Green Mile execution event. Stay safe out there, and may the fittest survive."

Her tone is about as shitty as my mood.

I appreciate that.

"All rise," Elliott says in his most authoritative voice, which is fucking ridiculous—not only because he's a shit actor, but also because we're all already standing.

Governor Steele stands and almost knocks his microphone off the podium with his belly when he turns to leave. I can't believe this piece of shit is the one who decides whether I live or die.

Decided.

Fuck me.

Once the camera crew leaves, Officer Elliott blows out a breath and folds at the waist like he just ran a marathon. "Good Lawd! If I had to suck my stomach in for one more minute, I was gonna fall out on the floor!"

Ramirez and Riggins, the two cops who brought me in yesterday, chuckle as they head past us toward the door.

"You deserve an Emmy for that performance, Elliott," Ramirez taunts.

"Pssh. Please. I deserve a Oscar!" He flips his nonexistent hair over his shoulder as the two glorified beat cops laugh their way to the exit.

Elliott's smiling eyes land on me, and suddenly, they're not so smiley anymore.

"You deserve a Oscar too," he says, his mouth forming a flat line. "You did good, handsome."

I give him the same bored expression I gave Governor Fuckface and let him lead me by the elbow out the door, down a metal staircase, and through the underground tunnel that connects the courthouse to the police station across the street.

While Elliott fills the silence with tales about all the celebrity trials he's done, I find myself analyzing the path of the pipes and air-conditioning vents overhead, the placement of the lights and security cameras, the weapons holstered on Elliott's belt.

"Most actors are short as hell in person, but Chris Tucker? Ooh…now, that's a tall drink of water! Nice, too! Have you ever seen *The Fifth Element*? When I saw that movie, I told my mama I wanted to be Ruby Rhod when I grew up!"

As we climb the stairs that lead up to the police station, I find myself analyzing Elliott as well. At first, I thought he was just filling the silence because he's a self-absorbed, narcissistic star-fucker, but when he glances at me, there's a sadness in his eyes that tells me he's not trying to impress me.

He's trying to distract me.

Because I was just sentenced to fucking death, and the only thing he can do about it is try to take my mind off of it for a few minutes.

When we get back to my cell, Elliott pats me on the back. "Okay, my man. Officer Hoyt will be back with your dinner in a few minutes. You green?"

"Super green," I mumble, walking through the open bars.

"Ha! I knew you'd seen that movie! You got Korben Dallas written alllll over you, honey!" Elliott beams as he closes the door and gestures for me to turn around and stick my hands through the bars.

On second thought, maybe this asshole wasn't trying to make me feel better, I think as I face the wall and let Elliott take off my handcuffs and shackles. *Maybe he was trying to make* himself *feel better.*

Guilt. I can work with that.

"How did your sentencing go, friend?" Doug asks from the cell next to me. His voice is raw and tired.

I groan as Elliott walks away, twisting my sore wrists in front of me. "It fuckin' went."

"I'm sorry."

"It is what it is."

There's a silence, and then Doug clears his throat. "Officer Hoyt's bringing me my last meal soon. They let me choose between the chicken Alfredo and beef Wellington."

Fuck, man.

Doug's trying to sound tough, and for some reason, that makes it even worse.

I swallow the lump forming in my throat and ask, "What'd you go with?"

"The beef," he says with a sniffle. "My wife never let me eat red meat." His voice breaks at the mention of his girl, erupting into the kind of sob that's so painful it doesn't make a sound. Only gasps and gurgles and deep, guttural moans.

I let my head fall back against the cinder-block wall and close my eyes, but I don't fucking cry.

Because unlike Doug, I'm gonna see my girl again.

I thought I could do this.

I thought I had changed.

I thought I could sacrifice myself for her and make God happy for once in my shitty waste of a life.

But fuck that.

If God wanted a martyr, he shouldn't have chosen a motherfucker who knows how to pick locks with a plastic fork.

Rain

OUR GARAGE DOESN'T HAVE windows.

My garage.

Their garage.

Their garage doesn't have windows.

It's pitch-black in here, day or night.

I don't know which one it is anymore.

The sound of cockroaches scurrying around makes me think it must be getting dark outside. They usually only come out at night.

Thank God I have my boots on.

Not that I can feel my feet anyway. I haven't been able to straighten my legs for hours. Sophie dragged a chair from the dining room out here, and Carter duct-taped me to it. He bound my ankles to the wooden legs and taped my wrists to the armrests.

Now I can't feel my hands either.

I spent the first hour or two tugging on my restraints, trying to shuffle my chair across the floor without making noise, trying to think of something in here that I could use as a tool or a weapon, but once my anger wore off, I remembered that it doesn't really matter.

What's the point of escaping when you have nowhere else to go?

This used to be my home.

Then, Wes became my home.

And now … I'm just homeless.

I picture Wes's face, bitter but not broken, defiant but not desperate, as he stood before the governor. Since the moment they ripped him away from me, I've thought of him as dead. But he's not. I looked at him, and he looked at me. And somehow, that makes it hurt more. Knowing he's out there and I can't get to him. Touching his cheek and feeling nothing but dust and static beneath my fingers. Knowing that he's locked in a cell somewhere, while I'm locked in one of my own.

If the tables were turned, Wes would come for me. I know he would. He would storm the castle and slay the dragons and burn the entire kingdom to the ground to save me.

But no one's coming for him.

And the saddest part is that no one ever has.

The door to the kitchen swings open, and I wince when the overhead fluorescent lights come on. Squeezing my eyes shut, I try to bury my face in my shoulder to hide from the unbearable brightness.

"Dinnertime." Mrs. Renshaw's voice is raspy but strong as she drags another dining room chair across the cement floor.

I hear the click-clack of high heels and the crinkle of a paper bag, which I assume holds the French fries and greasy hamburger I'm smelling.

Once my eyes adjust to the light, I blink them a few times and find Mrs. Renshaw sitting directly across from me—legs crossed, pantyhose on, wig smoothed down, jewelry for days. She glares at me like I'm in an interrogation room, and with this lighting, I might as well be.

Mrs. Renshaw places a Styrofoam to-go cup in my right hand, which is still lashed to the armrest, and then rips the piece of duct tape covering my mouth off in one swift motion, taking the skin off of my dry, chapped lips along with it.

I open and close my mouth, working my sore jaw. Then, I lean forward and take a huge slurp from the red plastic to-go cup straw. Cool water fills my mouth, but it could be gasoline for all I care. I haven't had anything to drink all day.

"Let's get one thing straight," Mrs. Renshaw says, her penciled-on eyebrows arching to the heavens as she leans forward, wrapping her forearms around the bag in her lap. "I ain't sorry for what I done. You can be mad at me all you want, Rainbow, but I will never apologize for trying to protect my family." She drops her eyes to my belly. "One day, when you're a mama, you'll understand."

A wistful smile tugs at the corners of her glossy lips before she sits up straighter and furrows her brows at me. "I always thought of you as one of my own. I loved you like you was family. But I was wrong about you." She wags her finger at me like I'm sitting in the principal's office. "You are no child of mine. You are yo' daddy's child through and through. Evil. Violent. Disturbed. Just like your savage friend who attacked my boy."

I squeeze the to-go cup in my fist, digging my fingernails into the Styrofoam until I feel tiny streams of cool water running down the sides of my fingers and over my palm. When the water reaches my wrist, I get an idea.

"You're carryin' my grandbaby, so I can't turn you in, but … I can't let you come near me or my family again either."

Mrs. Renshaw reaches into the bag and pops a handful of French fries into her mouth, closing her eyes as she savors the food just to torture me. Luckily, it gives me an opportunity to twist my wrist back and forth to help the moisture make its way underneath the duct tape.

"So, I decided"—Mrs. Renshaw swallows her mouthful of fried potato and licks the salt from her freshly painted fingertips—"I'm gon' keep you out here till the baby's born."

"What?"

Her lined lips curl into a sneer as she takes in my horrified expression. "Don't worry; we'll find you somethin' to sleep on and a place to do your business, which, honestly, is more than you deserve."

Mrs. Renshaw digs around in the bag again. The crinkling sound masks the noise the tape makes when I give my wrist one final twist, breaking the adhesive bond. Water runs down my forearm and drips out the other side of the tape, causing a jolt of fear to surge through me. I hold my breath and shift my hips in my seat just in time to catch the stream on my thigh. It lands on my jeans almost silently, and I exhale.

Leaning forward, I pretend to take another sip from the cup, holding it in place with my chin so that I can let go of it with my hand. I manage to wriggle it free from the now-useless tape as Mrs. Renshaw swallows another mouthful of fries.

"Now …" she mumbles, rummaging in the bag and pulling out a King Burger wrapped in shiny yellow paper. She peels the wrapper back on one side and holds it toward me. "Open up and say—ahh!"

Mrs. Renshaw lets out a shriek as my to-go cup flies toward her face, spraying water in all directions like a loose fire hose. She drops the food and squeezes her eyes shut, shielding herself with her hands. It buys me just enough time to reach into the back of my jeans, grab my Daddy's Beretta, and hit her upside the head with it as hard as I possibly can.

Her eyes snap to mine but only for a split second before they glaze over and roll up under her eyelids. Mrs. Renshaw slumps sideways in her chair, knocking over the Burger Palace bag along the way. Golden fries spill onto the oil-stained floor as I clutch the gun between my thighs and struggle to unwrap my left wrist.

Mrs. Renshaw moans and makes a smacking sound with her mouth as I free my left hand and start on the tape around my ankles.

The moaning gets louder as I free my right foot, but when I go to work on the other side, a hand shoots out and grabs my wrist.

I scream and try to pull my arm away, but all that does is jerk her body closer to me. Mrs. Renshaw is still slumped over sideways, and her wig has fallen halfway off, but her eyes are open and trying to focus on me. A trickle of blood flows from her temple down to the corner of her eye, turning the white part bright red. Then, it darts from my face to the gun between my legs.

Shit!

Her grip around my wrist tightens violently as she strains with her free hand to grab the weapon. My heart pounds like a desperate fist against my ribs as I snatch the gun out of her reach. Then, it stops completely as I bring it down like a hammer on the top of her head.

Crack.

Mrs. Renshaw's body goes limp, landing in my lap before sliding down my legs to the floor.

Oh God.

I roll her off my feet so that I can free myself. The Burger Palace bag crinkles loudly underneath her, and my stomach growls. Once the duct tape is off, I hold my breath and roll her onto her side, pulling the pulverized burger out from under her lifeless body.

I know I should check for a pulse, but I … I just can't.

She's fine, I tell myself as I shove the flattened sandwich into my hoodie pocket. *She's gonna be fine.*

Running over to the wall, I reach up to hit the automatic garage door button, but the sound of Wes's voice stops my hand in midair.

"Supplies. Shelter. Self-defense."

I picture his face the way it looked on the morning of April 24, when we woke up and realized that the world hadn't ended after all. His exhausted green eyes, bloodshot and rimmed with red. His battle-worn face, covered in dirt and ash and stubble. His blue Hawaiian shirt, smeared with Quint's blood. And I hear his pep talk again, too, but this time, I listen. I really listen.

"All you gotta do is say, Fuck 'em, *and survive anyway,"* he said, wiping the tears from my filthy cheeks. *"That's it. First, you say,* Fuck 'em. *Then, you figure out what you need to survive. So … figure it out. What do you need today?"*

"Food," I whisper to myself.

"Good. Do you have any?"

I picture my tree house full of cans and vitamins and nod.

"Supplies … check. What else do you need?"

"A way to get to you," I mumble, dropping my forehead to the wall next to the garage door button.

"A vehicle. That can be your shelter, too. What else?"

"An army to help me get you out."

"That would be nice, but let's start with …" I picture Wes tapping the handle of the revolver sticking out of his shoulder holster with a smirk.

"My daddy's gun," I sigh.

"Self-defense. Supplies, shelter, and self-defense. That's all you need."

I remember the way Wes smiled at me after that little speech. His tired green eyes didn't even crease at the corners. There was a sadness in them I'd never seen before. A resignation that made me nervous.

"See?" he said, letting his fake grin fall as two miserable mossy eyes stared right through me. "You got this."

"No," I corrected him. "We got this."

I don't know if I believe those words any more than I did on April 24, but I take a deep breath and push open the kitchen door anyway.

Because Mrs. Renshaw was right.

When you're a mama, you really will do anything to protect your family.

And Wes is all the family I got.

Rain

I OPEN THE DOOR just a crack and listen for people inside. Footsteps, drawers opening, anything to help me figure out whether or not the coast is clear. The house is eerily still other than the sound of a man's muffled voice in the distance. I can't make out what he's saying, but his Southern drawl and grandstanding tone make me think it must be Mr. Renshaw … until the phrase, "violatin' the laws of Mutha Naychuh," rises above the white noise.

Governor Steele.

My heart sinks. They're probably all gathered around the TV, watching today's execution.

And tomorrow, they could be watching Wes's.

No! The thought practically pushes me through the door into the kitchen. My guilt over what I just did to Mrs. Renshaw dissipates when I see what she's done to the place.

Mama's watercolor landscapes that used to hang on the wall in the breakfast nook, the stained-glass sun catchers I made as a kid that she had propped up in the window, her collection of fridge magnets from places other people had visited—all gone. Now, it's nothing but roosters. Everywhere. A metal rooster crossing sign, stained black from the flames that destroyed her own kitchen. Ceramic rooster cookie jars with the glaze all melted off. Glass rooster salt and pepper shakers that are so cracked they couldn't hold a grain of either one. Mrs. Renshaw must have dug every damn rooster she could find out of the ashes of her kitchen and shoved them all in here.

A hate I have never felt before begins to swirl inside of me. I exhale it through my nose like dragon smoke. It seeps through my pores like steam from a hot sidewalk. It clouds my vision, turning everything I see as red as the comb on a rooster's head.

It takes all of my self-control to stay silent as I walk over to the breakfast table. I want to stomp and growl and rip that metal sign off the wall so that I can use it to smash every other rooster in this room. But I breathe through my mouth and avoid the squeakiest floorboards as I tiptoe over to Mrs. Renshaw's purse on the kitchen counter. It's a big, ugly sack of a thing with rhinestones all over it, but when I lift the flap and look inside, a crystal rooster keychain stares back at me … along with a key fob that says *GMC* on the back of it.

I close my eyes and say, *Thank you*, but I don't know who I think is listening.

Mama maybe?

It can't be God. He deserted us months ago.

Opening the drawer next to the oven as quietly as possible, I reach in and take out the can opener.

"Bailiff! Bring out the accused!"

Crap!

The execution's almost over. I have to hurry. I close the drawer and slide the can opener into Mrs. Renshaw's purse, and then I slowly lift the bag off the counter. I make sure that nothing inside jingles or rattles as I drape the strap over my neck and across my body. Then, I turn.

And find Sophia Elizabeth Renshaw staring at me from five feet away.

"How did you—"

I dart forward and wrap my hand around her mouth, peeking into the dining room and up the few stairs to the living room where her dad and brother are staring with wide eyes at the glowing screen.

POW!

They both jump in their seats as I pull my head back into the kitchen.

"Sweetie …" I scramble to come up with an explanation that will make sense to a ten-year-old, but as I stare into her deep brown eyes, wide with fear and confusion and blind trust, all I can think to say is, "I love you. So much. Don't ever forget that."

Sophie blinks twice and then nods a little into my hand.

"I have to go now. Do me a favor and don't tell the guys you saw me, okay? They'll be mad."

Sophie nods again, pulling her eyebrows together, and I drop to my knees to hug her.

"Once again, I'm Michelle Ling, reporting live from Plaza Park. Today's Green Mile execution event was brought to you by Garden Warehouse. On behalf of Governor Steele and the great state of Georgia, stay safe out there, and may the fittest survive."

"Dude," Carter groans from the living room. "They have *got* to start making those holes bigger. Did you see the way that guy smacked his head on the way down? Ugh." I hear the squeak of my couch cushions and know my time is up.

"Don't s'pose it matters now, does it?" Mr. Renshaw replies as I give Sophie one last squeeze.

I can't leave through the back door in the dining room because they'll see me, so I turn and tiptoe back over to the garage, pressing my finger to my lips as Sophie watches me go.

I slide through the door and close it behind me with the quietest click, relieved to see that Mrs. Renshaw's body is right where I left it.

But horrified to see a spot of blood forming on the concrete next to her head.

My stomach lurches violently, but there's nothing in it to throw up.

I realize that if I hit the garage door button, Jimbo and Carter will hear that rusty old motor and come running, and I need more time if I'm gonna grab my supplies out of the tree house.

That only leaves me with one choice.

I have to open it myself.

Pressing my vanilla-scented hoodie sleeve to my mouth and nose, I tiptoe over to the chair where I spent most of the day restrained in the dark and climb up onto it.

Don't look down. Don't look down. Don't look down, I think as I teeter over Mrs. Renshaw's lifeless body and reach for the emergency release cord hanging from the metal track above my head. I tug on it, like Wes did on April 23 when we had no power and needed to get Mama's motorcycle out of the garage, but it's stuck. So, using both hands, I yank on the cord as hard as I can.

The release mechanism pops open, knocking me off-balance and causing my feet—and the chair—to come out from under me. I swing from the cord wildly, legs flailing and teeth gritted as I wait for the crash, but it never comes. Just a soft *thud*. I realize before I even drop to my feet what must have broken my chair's fall.

Agnes Renshaw.

I don't even look as I dart past her and hoist the heavy garage door up by hand. Then, once I duck underneath and slide it back down, I tear around the side of the house and through the backyard. The sun is setting behind the trees, but there's enough light left that anybody who happens to be looking out a window right now would see me dashing up my tree house ladder. All I can do is hurry and pray that they don't.

I chuck all of the cans and vitamin bottles back into the Huckabee's Foods bags and give my parents one last glance as I sprint through the knee-high grass toward the front yard. The wind chimes on the back porch tell me goodbye as I round the side of the house. I pass my daddy's rusted old truck and Mama's motorcycle—that hopefully no one here knows how to drive—and set my sights on the silver GMC at the top of the driveway.

With my heart in my throat, I reach out and grab the driver's side door handle, seconds away from being home free, but instead of feeling the door unlatch and swing open, I feel resistance followed by sheer terror when the headlights begin to blink, and the horn begins to blare.

Shit, shit, shit!

I scramble to shift all the bags I'm carrying to one hand as I dig in Mrs. Renshaw's purse for the car key with my other. I glance at the window next to the front door where I can see Carter and Jimbo on the other side, sitting on the couch, facing the TV. Both of their heads turn in my direction, and Carter shoots to his feet.

Come on!

My thumb grazes the jagged comb on the crystal rooster's head as the front door swings wide open. Carter's furious gaze lands on me as I yank the keychain out and frantically begin mashing buttons. I tug on the door handle and push and push and push every rubbery square as Carter leaps down my front porch stairs and runs at full speed up my driveway. The door finally flies open, and I dive inside, slamming it shut just as Carter's fingers wrap around the edge of it. He screams as I pull harder and harder, trying to get the door to latch. The moment it does, I hit the lock button and jam the key into the ignition.

"You bitch!" Carter screams, cradling his smashed fingers while he kicks the side of the truck, but I don't look at him.

I shift into reverse and peel out of there, feeling a bump under my tire just before Carter screams again.

I risk one last glance at the house as I shift into drive. Mrs. Renshaw is in the garage, facedown under a wooden chair. Carter is hopping on one foot in the driveway, screaming every swear word he knows at the top of his lungs. Mr. Renshaw is standing on the front porch, using the railing as a crutch while he shakes his head in disappointment. And above the garage, where the blinds on my bedroom window are spread apart, I'm sure two big brown eyes are watching me go.

I tear my gaze away from that house of horrors and focus solely on the double yellow line stretching out before me.

"I ain't sorry for what I done."

Well, Agnes, that makes two of us.

Rain

FRANKLIN HIGHWAY CUTS THROUGH the hundred-foot-tall Georgia pines like it's always been there. The smooth curves and rolling hills help calm me down, much like the glowing blue lights on the instrument panel of Mr. Renshaw's fancy new truck. There's one red light that catches my attention, and as soon as my brain is able to process information again, I slam on the brakes and come to a screeching stop right in the middle of the highway.

"Oh my God," I mutter, lowering the parking brake that I've driven over five miles without realizing was still on.

My hands shake as I wrap them around the steering wheel again, and I wonder if it's from adrenaline or hunger. Probably both. I pull the flattened burger out of my hoodie pocket and peel back the crumpled yellow paper. It looks like roadkill, but my mouth waters at the sight of it anyway.

I devour it as I drive downhill through the darkening woods, careful to avoid all the twisted metal and broken glass that Quint's bulldozer didn't clear.

Quint.

I wonder how he and Lamar are doing.

Stuck at the mall with that psychopath, Q.

I bet she's gonna make 'em scout for her now that Wes is gone.

Oh God. They won't last five minutes outside of the mall. The Bonys are gonna eat them alive.

The truck's headlights illuminate a charred, blackened bulldozer up ahead, right in front of the mangled, overturned eighteen-wheeler that exploded when Quint and Lamar tried to push it out of the way. Visions of yellow sparks and orange flames flicker before me in my mind. The sound of flying debris landing all around us fills the quiet cab. My heart begins to race as I remember finding Quint and Lamar, unresponsive in the wreckage, blanketed with broken glass. And when I pull off onto the Pritchard Park Mall exit ramp, I know what I have to do even before I drive over the flattened chain-link fence surrounding the mall.

The whole reason Wes was sentenced to death is because he helped me save Quint's life.

If I leave him here, if Q makes him start scouting, all of that will be for nothing.

I turn my headlights off as I drive across the empty parking lot, pulling up to the curb directly in front of the main entrance. If I didn't know better, I'd think this place was just as abandoned as it had been when they boarded it up ten years ago. But I do know better. There's a whole community of armed runaways living inside, a whole farm's worth of food growing on the roof, and a whole pecking order of power that starts with Q and ends with whoever is at the bottom dying at the hands of Bonys while trying to fulfill her list of demands.

I shut off the ignition, pocket the key, and pull the gun out of my waistband. Taking a deep breath, I look around to make sure there isn't a murderous, spray-painted motorcycle gang coming my way. Then, I hop out of the truck, lock the doors behind me, and dash inside.

The building is dark and dank and smells like mildew. The sound of frogs croaking and crickets chirping echoes in the atrium up ahead, and the filthy, cracked floor tiles clatter under my boots. I can't believe I considered this place home just a few days ago. I was so blinded by my fear of the outside world that I couldn't see it for what it was.

A disgusting, disintegrating hellhole.

I creep down the darkened hallway and pull the gun out from my waistband, wishing it were a flashlight instead. I peek my head into the tuxedo rental shop where Quint and Lamar have been living ever since the accident, but no one's home.

They're probably in the food court, finishing dinner.

I consider waiting for them here to avoid a conflict with Q, but that thought lasts half a second before my feet turn and carry me straight toward the cafeteria.

Wes could be executed as soon as tomorrow. Time is a luxury I don't have.

The sounds of laughing, shouting, accordion-playing, and obnoxious singing get louder and louder as I make my way through the atrium, past the crumbling fountain—with its murky water and random swamp plants—and around the broken escalators. I remember when the idea of seeing Q used to scare me to the point that I wouldn't leave the tuxedo shop, but that feels like a lifetime ago. Back when my only goal was to avoid my own pain.

Well, there's no avoiding it now. It's here. It's in my face and in my house and on my TV and buried in my backyard.

Q can't hurt me worse than this.

Just before I walk through the food court doors, I shove the gun back into my waistband and cover it with Carter's hoodie. I don't want to cause trouble. I just want to get my friends and get the hell out of Pritchard Park. Forever.

The burn barrel in the center of the cavernous room is still smoking from tonight's dinner, but nobody is manning it.

Everyone is at their designated spots—Q and the runaways are at the back table, living it up like they're at the Mad Hatter's tea party, and the Jones brothers are sitting by themselves at a table off to the right, picking at their almost empty plates in silence. It's weird to see the Renshaws' table empty, but I refuse to think about them right now.

Or ever again.

I glance at Q as I tiptoe across the room. Her head is thrown back in laughter. A cloud of pot smoke swirls above her head. She doesn't see me … yet.

But Brangelina does. Brad and Not Brad elbow each other and jerk their prominent chins at me as I tear my eyes away and focus on what I came here to get.

Quint's face lights up as I approach their table. Where there was once a shard of glass four inches long sticking out of the side of his neck, he now sports a single bandage. The beige color stands out against his dark skin.

Lamar turns his head but doesn't give me the same warm welcome as his brother. He glares at me like I'm just one more mother figure who abandoned them, his fifteen-year-old authority problem stronger than ever.

"What are you doing here?" Quint asks, wincing as he tries to turn his neck to look in Q's direction.

"I'll tell you in the truck," I whisper, crouching down next to their table. "C'mon. Let's go before the queen decides to—"

"Ho. Lee. Shit," a raspy voice announces from the back of the room. "Look what the fuck the cat dragged in, y'all."

I sigh and stand up. Turning to face Q, I hold my head up but keep my posture loose, like Wes did as he faced the judge today.

Q stands and steps onto her chair before walking across the table and leaping down to the floor with the smug swagger of an untouchable kingpin. Her baggy black men's T-shirt and dress pants, cut off at the knee, hang from her curves like high fashion as she tosses her faded green dreadlocks over her shoulder and levels me with an amused stare.

"I knew as soon as I saw Surfer Boy on TV today that yo' ass would come crawlin' back to Mama Q, and here you is. Couldn't even make it a day on ya own, huh, princess?" Q stalks toward me like a jungle cat, but I hold my ground.

"I'm not here to stay. I just came back to get my friends."

"You mean, you came back to snatch my scouts." Her tone turns venomous as she moves in closer.

"Q, please," I plead. "Just let them go. Wes scouted more than enough supplies to cover all four of our shares while he was here."

"Well, he ain't here no more, now is he?"

"No!" I shout, feeling my face get hot. "He's not! And if you don't let us go, you're gonna get to watch him die on live TV in two days!" I shove my finger in the direction of the fast-food menu screens lining the left side of the food court.

Q's dark eyebrows shoot up as she reaches out and grabs my face with her right hand. Her chunky silver rings collide with the fading bruise on my cheekbone, and her long, sharp fingernails dig into my flushed skin.

"Bitch," she hisses, baring her teeth, "you done fucked up fo' da last time. You think you can come up in *my* castle and talk shit to *the queen*?" Sinking her talons even deeper into my flesh, Q drags me by the face toward the food court entrance. "Errybody say, *Bye, bitch.*"

"Bye, bitch!" a chorus erupts behind us, followed by laughing and clanking and banging around.

I squeal into her palm, but she only tightens her grip on my face. My skin splits in all five places where her nails stab into it. I wrap my hands around her wrist—not to pull her hand away, but to pull it closer. Q cackles as she walks backward in front of me, dragging me down the hall, completely at her mercy. I consider pulling my gun out, but if Q saw me reach for my waistband, she'd probably grab my gun and stick it down my throat before I could even get a hand on it.

I grunt in frustration and dig my own nails into her wrist.

"Ow!" She jerks my face violently, opening the wounds even more. "Calm the fuck down, ho!"

"Let me go!" I scream, but it comes out as three muffled syllables against her palm.

Suddenly, Q shoves me away from her, and I land with a surprisingly soft thud. I open my eyes and find myself in a small room, sprawled out on a mattress on the floor. Q reaches behind a counter, and with a quiet *click*, a few strands of battery-powered Christmas lights come on. They snake back and forth across the ceiling, illuminating the small space just enough to indicate that it must have been a tiny boutique once, maybe even a candle store or a tobacco shop. Now, it just houses a wooden counter where the register once was, a mattress on the floor covered in black bedding, and an entire wall of shelves that now hold all of Q's personal belongings.

Out of every store in the entire mall, I never would have pictured her choosing such a cozy, modest spot to claim as her bedroom.

I scramble to my feet and reach for my gun, but Q beats me to it, pulling hers out even faster.

"Goddamn, you suck at this. Put it in the *front* of yo' pants or somethin'. I coulda shot yo' ass fifteen times by now."

"Why haven't you?" I snap.

"'Cause it's mo' fun to fuck wit' you than it would be to mop you up." She shoves her gun back into the pocket of her baggy shorts and smirks. "Put that thing down, bitch. You ain't gonna shoot nobody."

I sigh and wrestle the gun into the front of my jeans, the waistband already starting to feel a little bit tighter than usual.

Q walks behind the checkout counter and opens a cabinet underneath. "You really gon' try to bust Surfer Boy outta jail?"

"Um … yeah. I guess." I shrug, losing confidence by the second.

"Good. Here." A pink bundle flies across the room, hitting me square in the chest.

I groan as I catch it, smelling a hint of cigarette smoke and hazelnut coffee wafting off the shiny fabric.

"Is this … my duffel bag?" I hold it out and look it over in the dim light. I haven't seen it since Carter dumped it out in front of Q yesterday—*God, was that only yesterday?*—when he tried to bust Wes for hoarding supplies. It feels like everything must still be in here.

"Take ya shit, and go get my boy. Hawaii Five-Oh's too damn pretty to get turned into muhfuckin' plant food." Q shakes her head with sincerity. "Best scout I eva had."

I don't even know what to say. I thought she was going to kill me—or at least beat the crap out of me—and here she is … helping me?

"What about Quint and Lamar?"

"Who, them?" Q flicks her chin at something over my shoulder.

I turn my head to find the Jones brothers standing on the other side of the hall, huddled together but still watching my back.

"I ain't got no use for those pussies. I *hope* you fuckin' take 'em."

"But you said—"

"Listen, bitch. I said what I said 'cause you was disrespectin' me in front of my crew. I snatched ya face 'cause you was disrespectin' me in front of my crew. But the truth is, the faster y'all get the fuck up out my castle, the betta. I got enough mouths to feed."

"Thank you, Q. Really. I don't—"

"Eh, eh, eh, eh," she cuts me off with an aggravated wave of her hand. "Get the fuck outta here. Go on now, 'fore I change my mind and shoot yo' ass."

I nod at the dreadlocked lioness and turn around to claim my last remaining friends.

Quint's and Lamar's eyes go wide as I walk out of the queen's lair with blood dripping down my face and a pink duffel bag in my arms.

"Y'all wanna take a ride downtown?" I ask with an exhausted smile.

"Fuck yeah!" Lamar punches the air in front of him.

"You sure about this?" Quint asks, his eyebrows pulling together as we turn and walk toward the main entrance.

"Quint," I warn. "Without Wes, you'd be—"

"I know; I know. I'm in. I just wanna make sure you thought about—oh shit. Look!" Quint raises a finger, and I follow his stare down the hall to the main entrance doors.

Right outside, perfectly visible through all the panes of missing glass, a swarm of Bonys has descended upon the Renshaws' truck like it's a two-ton piñata. Hoots and hollers and glass breaking and metal smashing echo down the corridor as they take their crowbars and spray-paint cans and steel-toed boots to the massive GMC.

"No!" I scream, shoving my duffel bag into Lamar's arms as I take off running down the hallway.

"Rain! Stop!"

But I can't. This is the moment when Wes would chastise me for being "impulsive." Yell at me for "not listening." Tell me I have "a death wish." But Wes isn't here. And the only hope I have of getting to him before he's *not here* for good is that damn truck.

Crash!

A man in a leather jacket and a motorcycle helmet with nails drilled through it from the inside out smashes the driver's side window as his buddy in a zombified clown mask spray-paints the words *DEATH TO SHEEP* in two-foot-tall letters on the side of the dented white truck. A third guy wearing a *Scream* mask climbs up onto the hood and holds a crowbar over his head in a stabbing motion aimed at the windshield. All three of them have on black jackets with neon-orange skeleton bones spray-painted on them.

"Stop!" I scream, pushing through the exit door and waving my hands in the air. "Stop! Stop! Stop!"

My hands drop to my sides in relief when they actually do stop, but then my heart climbs into my throat as I look for an escape route when all three of their heads turn toward me like snakes spotting a mouse.

"Please," I say, holding my hands up. "There's a purse on the passenger seat. Take it. Take whatever you want, just … please leave the truck."

Pinhead and the undead clown glance at each other with a chuckle, which turns into full-blown maniacal laughter as they turn and walk toward me in unison.

"Take whatever we want, huh?" the guy with the nails sticking out of his helmet asks with a snaggletooth sneer.

The rotting clown makes a slurping sound as he flicks his tongue in and out of the rubbery mouth hole on his mask.

I don't even realize I've been walking backward until my heel hits one of the metal doors behind me.

"Whoa!" the guy in the *Scream* mask exclaims from somewhere near the truck.

His friends turn, and I watch as he pulls my dad's Smith & Wesson revolver out of Agnes's purse. She must have stashed it in there after she swiped it from me yesterday.

"Holy shit, bro!" Pinhead exclaims. "That looks like the gun from *Dirty Harry*!"

"Who the fuck carries a .44 Magnum?" The creepy clown chuckles. "Fuckin' thing weighs, like, six pounds and only shoots six bullets!"

The guy holding the revolver lifts his mask to reveal the rounded baby face of a kid no older than Lamar. But these guys don't treat him like a kid. They step aside so that he can approach me, eyes narrowed, gears turning.

"I know a dude who carries a gun just like this," he says, lifting the revolver in his hand. "You know him?"

I don't have to ask who he's talking about. There's a sadness in his tone, a fondness, a sense of loss that I recognize.

"Yeah." I nod, this single ounce of compassion making my chest ache and my eyes sting.

"I saw him on TV today," the kid says, softening his tone.

"Oh shit! The nerd?" Pinhead asks.

"No, dumbass," the boy snaps back. "The dude from the sentencing. He was the one who used to come into the CVS all the time and pay me in hydro."

"Ohhhh, that guy. Yeah, he cool."

"That's …" I clear my throat, hoping they won't hear my voice shaking. "That's why I need the truck. I'm gonna go to the capitol, and … I don't know … try to …" I can't even say it out loud. It sounds so stupid. It is stupid.

But it wouldn't be if I had help.

"Hey … you guys could come too." I try to smile, but it feels like a grimace. "Since you knew him. *Know* him, I mean. You could help me—"

The zombified clown snorts into his rubber mask as his helmeted buddy erupts into hysterics.

"Do we look like muhfuckin' customer service to you?" The clown chuckles.

"Yeah," Pinhead blurts out through his hyena-like laughter, clicking his heels together and giving me a salute. "Do we look like fuckin' Captain America and shit?"

As his friends keel over, laughing, the kid shakes his head and levels me with a sympathetic stare. "Listen, I'm sorry your man caught a case, but we ain't exactly in the helpin' business."

"We in the *stayin' the fuck alive* bidness, and bidness is gooood." The clown flicks his tongue at me again.

"Tell you what … I keep the bag, you keep the truck, and if anybody fucks with you"—the kid sets the purse and the gun on the hood of the GMC and picks up a can of orange spray paint one of them had tossed aside—"just tell 'em you're reppin' Pritchard Park."

I stand, petrified by a potent mixture of fear and shock and gratitude, as this Bony kid spray-paints stripes across my chest and down my arms to match his.

Dropping the can to the ground, the boy grabs Mrs. Renshaw's purse and climbs onto a motorcycle parked in front of the truck. He slides his *Scream* mask back into place and motions with his head for the two guys who had to be twice his age to follow.

"Dude"—the clown elbows Pinhead, and they walk over to their bikes—"did you see somebody spray-painted the highway sign to say Bitch-Ass Park?"

"Fuck yeah! I did that shit, man."

As the Bonys cackle and pull out of the parking lot on squealing tires, I stand like a newly decorated Christmas tree and wait for Quint and Lamar to come out from their hiding places.

When the door beside me finally squeaks open, Lamar is the one who speaks first, "I just want you to know, we totally had your back, Rainy Lady."

"A hundred percent," Quint chimes in.

"Just shut up and get in the truck," I snap.

"Yes, ma'am."

Wes

THE GREEN MILE. THAT'S what Officer MacArthur called it when he came to get Doug for his execution a few hours ago. After he sobbed all over his shitty fucking beef Wellington.

"*Time to walk the Green Mile, buddy.*"

Who says that? Heartless motherfucker. That must be why they sent him instead of Hoyt or Elliott. Those two still have some shred of humanity left. But Mac? He's older. Harder. His tightly cropped gray hair tells me he's probably ex-military, and the trench-deep lines around his eyes and mouth tell me that he's definitely seen some shit. That asshole looks like he eats nails for breakfast and tacks for snacks.

Speaking of nails, I've spent the last hour feeling around under my cot and the sink-slash-toilet unit in my cell, trying to find one.

As it turns out, I do not know how to pick a lock with a plastic fork.

I mean, I do—I had to do it all the time in foster home number ten. Or was it eleven? My foster mom wanted to keep her whole government check for herself, so she used to keep a lock on the fridge and the pantry to keep me from eating the good shit. All she left out was a loaf of generic white bread and a jar of government peanut butter.

So, I got real good at picking locks.

Before she kicked me out, of course.

As soon as Officer MacArthur left with Doug—poor fucking bastard—I knew I had a solid hour to get to work before everybody came back from the execution. They won't let you keep forks, for obvious reasons, but I managed to break one of the tines off without getting caught. That's all I needed to pick Ms. Irene's pantry lock, but the motherfucker on my holding cell is a beast. There's not a *single* mechanism you have to push inside—there are, like, five, and the fifth one is so far back I can't even reach it.

But maybe if I had a nail and figured out a way to bend the tip of it …

"What are you mopin' around fo'? I'm the one who had to walk his ass over to the hole!" Officer Elliott whines from somewhere down the hall.

I stand and quietly step toward the bars.

The mumbling I hear in response must be from Hoyt. He never talks much louder than a whisper. I can't make out a word he's saying.

"Mm-mm-mm. Pissed himself right there on live TV. What a gotdamn shitshow. I need a drink."

I hear the unmistakable rumble of a file cabinet drawer opening, followed by clinking glasses and a painful hiss that, after working in a dive bar for the last few months, I know was probably caused by a throatful of cheap whiskey.

"I think you need another one, big fella."

Clink.

Hiss.

"You know, when I got into this job, all I had to do was wear a uniform, walk some big, sexy men back and forth, listen to all that juicy drama in the courtroom, and collect my paycheck at the end of the month. I did *not* sign up for this shit."

Click.

Hiss.

Mumble. Mumble. Mumble.

"Right? Good benefits. Good retirement plan. Now, they got us killin' muhfuckas on the daily."

Mumble. Mumble.

"I know, hoss. They good folks. This shit ain't right."

Mumble. Mumble.

"You know what you need to do? You need to start workin' on yo' side hustle. Like me. I'mma get me some headshots done, get me a manager, a agent. What you gon' do?"

As Hoyt murmurs, I hear the file cabinet drawer close, and their voices grow louder as they move into the hallway. Elliott goes one way, and Hoyt heads toward me. I can tell it's him by the slow, heavy shuffling of his feet across the dirty floor. I lean against the bars and wait for him to pass.

When he does, he doesn't even look at me.

"Officer Hoyt?" I ask, using my least shitty tone.

Hoyt stops walking but keeps his eyes on the floor.

"I heard you guys talkin'. I just … I just want you to know that I don't blame you for … you know. Doing what you gotta do. You and Elliott, y'all are good dudes."

Hoyt doesn't say a word. He simply nods at the floor and keeps walking.

"Hey, Hoyt? Sorry, *Officer* Hoyt? Can I ask you a question?"

Hoyt stops again.

"You know how you let Doug choose his last meal? That was real nice, man. Meant a lot to him."

The big guy's chin drops almost to his chest, and I know I got him. It's shitty of me to prey on someone's kindness, but you know what else is shitty?

Being shot in the face on live TV.

"You know, I used to work in a bar, and we had last call. Everybody got one last drink before the bar closed for the night. It was good times, man. Some of the best times of my life. Anyway, I was wondering if, since I only got a day and half left, maybe I could get a drink. Like last call, you know? Somethin' strong, to take the edge off."

Hoyt shakes his head and staggers a little on his feet. He must have had more of that whiskey than I realized.

"Can't let ya have nuthin' glass in yer cell."

"Here. You can use this." I grab the plastic cup, with my toothbrush and comb inside, off the sink and shove it in between the bars, knocking the toothbrush to the body fluid–covered floor in the process.

"Shit."

I crouch down and pick up the toothbrush as Hoyt shuffles over.

"I'll get ya a new one," he mumbles, taking the cup from my outstretched hand as he glances up at the ceiling at the end of the hall.

A security camera. Of course.

"Thanks, man." I stand up, palming the toothbrush so that it's out of sight and hopefully out of mind. "You know, for what it's worth, Doug really did like you."

Hoyt finally looks at me, trying and failing to make eye contact as his glassy eyes swim in his bloated, ruddy face. He smells like a potent mixture of brown liquor and body odor, and I genuinely feel bad for the guy.

Just not as bad as I feel for myself.

He returns a few minutes later with a new cup and toothbrush.

"Got you a clean set," he mumbles, glancing at the camera and then back at his feet. "Wash up. It's gon' be lights out soon."

From the weight of the cup, I know as soon as he hands it to me that it's full of bottom-shelf whiskey, but that's not really what I was after.

What I wanted was an ally.

The spare toothbrush was just a bonus.

Rain

"IN ONE MILE, TURN right onto West Paces Ferry Road."

Evidently, Jimbo got all the bells and whistles when he bought this truck. It even has GPS built right into the dashboard. And thank God because even though I found my phone in the duffel bag Q gave me, it's dead as a doornail, and there was no way I'd have been able to find my way to downtown Atlanta with the back roads being as clogged up as they are.

"So … are you gonna tell us what's goin' on or what?" Quint asks, eyeing me suspiciously from the passenger seat.

"I already told you. We're going to get Wes."

"Not about that. I'm talkin' 'bout how your man beat the shit outta Carter yesterday; then Jimbo almost shot his ass and chased y'all outta the mall; then Agnes called the cops, and they took her to find you guys; then she came back *in this truck* to pick up Carter, Sophie, and Jimbo; and now, *you're* drivin' it even though they hate your ass right now."

"Oh. That." My mouth goes dry, and my palms begin to sweat as I think about the events that led up to me stealing this truck. I picture Agnes, facedown and bleeding in the garage. I picture sweet Sophie and Jimbo finding her there. Then, I picture Carter, sprinting up the driveway toward me, his mangled face twisted in rage.

I focus on the road in front of my headlights and try my best to breathe as I blink the unwanted images away. "The Renshaws stole my house, so I stole their truck."

I hope that's enough of an explanation for them, but of course, it's not.

"Stole your house? How the hell do you steal a house?" Lamar yells over the sound of the wind whipping through the busted-out windows from his spot on the tiny, fold-down backseat.

"They literally just moved in and took it over. I was too shocked and upset to fight back right away, but after I saw Wes's sentencing, I just … I don't know … I snapped. Agnes had Carter tie me up in the garage and said she was gonna keep me out there 'til the baby was born, but I escaped and stole their truck."

Quint's and Lamar's questions come rapid-fire after that.

"They tied you up?"

"The garage? Hell nah!"

"She was gonna keep you out there 'til *what* baby was born? The second coming of Christ?"

"Wait."

"Hold up."

"Are you …"

"No."

"You're *pregnant*?"

"Do you know who the daddy is?"

I glare at Lamar, who asked that last question.

"What?" He holds his hands up. "No shade. I probably got a coupl'a baby mamas out there I don't know about."

"Boy!" Quint reaches into the backseat and smacks Lamar upside the head. "You can't get a girl pregnant just by starin' at her, and that's about as far as you ever got."

"Pssh! You don't know my life. I got hos in different area codes."

"You been ridin' your bike to all those area codes? 'Cause you know you ain't got no license."

"It's Wes's," I snap, cutting them both off.

"Ohhhh shit." Quint's expression goes flat as he turns to face me again.

"Yeah."

"Sorry, Rain." Lamar drops his voice and gives me an awkward pat on the shoulder.

"Don't be sorry," I say, swerving to avoid a mangled muffler in the road. "Just help me get him out."

"Yes, ma'am." I see Lamar give me a little salute in the rearview mirror.

Quint nods in agreement.

Thankfully, the GPS lady chooses that exact moment to change the subject. "Turn right onto West Paces Ferry Road."

"Somebody should really make a post–April 23 GPS system," Lamar jokes. Then, he switches to his best robotic lady voice. "Turn right at the burning school bus."

Quint chuckles. "Or how 'bout, *Ignore that Stop sign unless you would like to be robbed at gunpoint.*"

I can't help but smile. Even Quint's GPS voice sounds Southern.

"I don't think we have to worry about getting robbed in a giant truck that says *DEATH TO SHEEP* on the side of it," I say, rolling my eyes.

"You know it probably just has dicks on the other side." Lamar laughs. "You can't give a dude a can of spray paint and *not* end up with a buncha dicks."

"Oh shit." Quint laughs, rummaging in the glove box until he finds a flashlight. Then, he leans out the broken passenger window and shines it on the side of the truck. "Gotdamn it! There's one right here on my door! Why does it hafta be on my side?"

We all laugh, which feels strange and wrong, considering the circumstances, before Quint pulls his head back into the truck.

"Jesus. Who the hell do you s'pose lives there?"

I follow his gaze out the window and find a house—no, a mansion—set back from the road behind a perfectly manicured lawn and a brightly lit fountain. The brick monstrosity is illuminated from all sides, making the white plantation-style columns—and the police cars lining the circular driveway—glow in the dark.

"That's the governor's mansion," Lamar says. "They didn't make y'all go there on a field trip?"

Quint and I shake our heads.

"Pssh. Y'all lucky. They made us go in sixth grade. Pissed me off so bad. How you gonna drag a buncha country kids all the way into the city just to show us a buncha shit we ain't never gonna have?"

"Yeah, especially when our tax money paid for all that shit," Quint adds, still staring out the window.

The property seems to go on forever.

"I didn't even learn nuthin'. 'Cept that Governor Steele has, like, thirty rooms in his house, a heated pool, a helicopter pad, some kinda marble floors that came from Italy or France or some-fuckin'-place. Oh, and at Christmastime every year, somebody makes a giant gotdamn four-foot-wide gingerbread house that looks just like the mansion, and then they just throw the whole thing away in January. Homeless people down the street would eat tha hell outta that thing!"

"And they say sharing what we got with sick people and old people is why we were facin' extinction. If you ask me, it was from assholes like this taking all the damn *resources* for themselves." Quint clicks off his flashlight and tosses it back into the glove box. "I saw on TV that one percent of the world's population owns ninety-nine percent of the wealth. If anything goes against nature, it's that shit."

"You're right." I nod, trying to keep my eyes on the road instead of the mansion my mama and daddy helped pay for with their hard-earned money. "I remember watchin' an episode of *Hoarders* once where they said that no other species on Earth hoards like humans do. I mean, animals will store food for winter or whatever, but they never take more than they actually need. Not like us."

By the time we get to the end of the property and pass the fully illuminated tennis court, I'm convinced that Governor Beauregard Steele's house is more than *anybody* actually needs.

"Turn left onto Northside Drive," the GPS lady says.

"How much longer?" Lamar whines from the backseat.

I glance at the glowing screen in the dashboard. "That's weird."

"What?"

"It says we're only nine miles away, but …"

"Ten hours?" Lamar yells, his face between Quint and me as he reads the dash for himself.

I assume it's a mistake until I come around a curve and have to jerk the wheel to avoid hitting a stopped car. The truck bounces as I careen over the curb and onto the grass, slamming on the brakes and coming to a stop inches away from a telephone pole.

Lamar flies into the dashboard and lands in Quint's lap. "What the hell, Rain?"

"Look!" I point through my broken window at the sea of parked cars stretching all the way down Northside Drive. At first, I assume there's just a bad wreck up ahead that never got cleared, but then I hear the sound of bass in the distance.

And screaming.

And gunshots.

The streetlights are still working, but that's more than I can say for the businesses lining the road. Smashed windows, busted neon signs … the bank has an actual car sticking out the side of it.

"We still have nine miles to go?" Quint asks.

"Uh-huh."

"There is heavier than expected traffic up ahead," the GPS lady announces.

"Yeah, no shit," Lamar grunts as he peels himself off the dash.

"I have an idea." I flip on the high beams and decide to try to drive down the side of the road. There are a few cars and mangled, twisted bumpers blocking the sidewalk, but I think I have just enough space to maneuver around them in the truck.

"Rain, are you sure we should go this way?" Quint asks.

The *br-r-r-r-ap* of a machine gun in the distance answers him with a resounding *no.*

"This is how the GPS said to go," I snap. "You got any better ideas?"

Quint shuts his mouth, and we creep alongside the road in silence, the sound of thumping hip-hop and excitement and fear and desperation growing louder with every passing second.

"Where is everybody?" Lamar asks, securely buckled in the backseat this time.

"I think we're about to find out."

We creep over the top of a hill, and the scene laid out before us looks like an anthill after it's been stepped on. There are people everywhere—fighting in the street, having sex in the street, standing on cars while watching other people fight and have sex in the street, shooting up in doorways, firing guns into the air, and walking around with homemade signs advertising whatever weapons, drugs, sex acts, or snacks they're selling.

I see two guys holding leashes and fistfuls of dollar bills while their pit bulls maul each other.

I see a guy pushing a grocery cart full of colorful bongs.

I see a man holding a machine gun, guarding a naked woman dancing on the corner in clear six-inch heels.

Then, I see a body lying facedown on the sidewalk in my headlights, and I have to slam on the brakes.

"Dude, are you crazy? You can't stop here," Lamar whines.

"I can't run her over either!"

"That bitch is already dead!"

"What if she isn't?"

"Maybe somebody should go check," Quint offers.

"One, two, three—"

"Not it!" We all shout in unison.

"Ahh! That was you, big bro! Go do it!"

"Whatever! We all said it at the same time!"

"Nuh-uh. You said it late."

"Ugh!" I groan. "*I'll* do it, okay?" I go to pull the gun out of my waistband when the sound of motorcycle engines perks my ears.

I lift my head and stare through the windshield as a group of neon-orange skeletons on motorcycles rushes down the street toward us like an approaching tidal wave. They crisscross between the parked cars, bashing them with baseball bats and shooting out their windshields with wolf-like howls.

Br-r-r-r-r-ap!

One of them mows down a group of semiconscious junkies leaning against a dumpster with a machine gun that's been mounted to the front of his motorcycle. Their bodies jerk and fall to the ground as screams fill the air. The folks on the street scatter like rats, diving for the alleys and huddling in vacant doorways.

"What the hell are y'all waitin' for? Let's go!" Lamar yells, pushing on the back of his brother's seat.

I reach out to grab my door handle when I notice the neon-orange bones painted on my sleeve.

"No," I mumble, letting go of the door.

"Rain!"

"Just ... just shut up, okay?" I wave Quint off while keeping my eyes locked on the leader of the pack. I couldn't look away if I wanted to.

"Fuck this!" Quint goes to open his door, but my hand shoots out and grabs a fistful of his T-shirt.

"The Bony kid said to tell 'em we're from Pritchard Park, remember? Maybe they can help us!"

Quint stares at me like I just sprouted a third eye. "Are you fuckin' crazy?"

"You're crazy if you think they aren't gonna shoot you the second you jump outta this truck!" I yell over the sound of approaching motorcycles and gunfire and howling.

It's so loud now I know they're on top of us … even before Quint's terrified eyes look past me and out the broken window.

"License and registration, ma'am," a sinister voice bellows in my ear.

With a deep breath, I turn and smile, which I realize a moment too late is the exact opposite of the hardened gangster vibe I was supposed to be going for. It's also the exact opposite of what I want to do when I take in the blood-spattered King Burger mask staring back at me. The eyes and nose have been painted black, and his grinning mouth has extra-white teeth painted on either side of it to resemble the lip-less smile of a skull. But instead of *Día de Muertos* designs painted on the cheeks and forehead, it's pot leaves and dollar signs. Not that I can see much of the forehead. The top half of the Bony's mask is shaded by the brim of an old velvet top hat, and his neon-orange bones have been spray-painted directly onto a fur coat that looks like it was made from the hides of a thousand calico cats. I can't really see his eyes, but I can *feel* them looking us over.

"Um …" I swallow. "We represent Pritchard Park?"

"Oh, do you now?"

The Bony's pack begins to surround the truck. I wince as the one on the dirt bike drives right over the woman on the sidewalk to position himself next to Quint's door.

"Mmhmm." My voice trembles as I force myself to stare into the black voids where his eyes should be.

"A'ight." He nods. His voice is calm—loud due to the engine noise but calm. Then, just as I begin to relax, he throws me a curveball.

"You say you a Bony bitch? Then, tell me … who's ya prez?"

My prez? Like, my president?

I assume he doesn't mean the president of the United States. It must be a biker-gang thing. Like who's my leader.

Crap.

My mind hurtles back in time to our run-in with the Pritchard Park Bonys. None of them mentioned any names, let alone the name of their leader. Come to think of it, I haven't seen any Bonys anywhere who seemed like leadership material.

Except for this guy.

"You?" I say, going out on a limb.

"You damn right!"

The masked man tips his head back and laughs. The sound allows me to breathe again. And sounds strangely familiar.

"What brings y'all to A-town?"

"I … uh …"

I glance at Quint, who looks like he's about to piss himself, but thankfully, Lamar pipes up from the backseat, trying to sound more hood than country, "Her baby daddy caught a case, yo. So, we goin' to the capitol to bust his ass out!"

"Ohhhh shiiiiiit!" The leader of the Bonys covers his toothy rubber mouth with a fist. Then, he offers it to Lamar for a bump. "Yo, Fat Sacks!" he yells to the Bony in front of the truck, wearing a black ski mask and a neck full of heavy gold chains. "These muhfuckas is gonna storm tha castle!"

The other Bony says something, but evidently, I'm not the only one who can't hear it because the prez shouts at him to repeat it. The gold-chain guy pulls up his ski mask and shouts louder, and everyone in the car gasps audibly.

"Holy shit!" Quint whisper-shouts.

"Is that Big Boi?" Lamar asks.

"From OutKast?" I squint, trying to get a better look at him before he pulls his ski mask back down. "No way."

Lamar, Quint, and I all turn to stare at The Prez in unison. I want to ask him if he's André 3000 so bad, but I also want to live, so I keep my mouth shut and pray that Lamar does the same for once in his life.

"It's y'alls' lucky day," The Prez announces, slapping the roof of the truck and making us jump. "My VP and his boys here are gonna give you cats a lift. It'd take y'all ten hours to get through this shit in that redneck mobile."

"Oh my God! That's what the GPS lady said!" Lamar whispers as Quint and I open our doors.

May 7
Wes

THREE HUNDRED FIFTY-FOUR cinder blocks, and not a damn one of them is even a little bit fucking loose.

I know because I stayed up all goddamn night, checking every single one.

The air vent is too small for a toddler to crawl through.

The floor is solid cement.

There are no fucking windows.

No fucking outlets.

And because the lock is unpickable without a bent nail, they put everything in here together with screws.

Out of options and ideas, I've been lying on my cot for the last few hours with my hands under my pillow, whittling the end of my bonus toothbrush into a spike, using the side of a screw. I don't want to have to hurt these guys. I actually kind of like them—well, except for Mac. But if it comes down to them or me …

"Mornin', sunshine. How you doin'?" Elliott calls from the hallway before appearing with a plastic tray. His smile fades as soon as he sees me. "Sorry. I guess that's a silly question, ain't it?"

I sit up, leaving the evidence of my shiv-making operation under my pillow, and scrub a hand down my face. "I was hoping I'd get some sleep with Doug bein' gone, but"—I shrug—"not so much."

Elliott shakes his head. "That was the cryin'-est damn man we eva had in here." He lifts a hand to the ceiling. "God rest his soul."

While Elliott reaches for his key, the rusty-ass gears in my brain slowly begin to turn again. "Since nobody took his spot, I guess this is a slow week for arrests, huh?"

"Why? You lookin' for a cellmate?" Elliott wiggles his eyebrows at me while he unlocks my door.

I know he's cracking jokes to keep things light, but heavy is the name of the game right now.

"Nah. I was just thinking, it's probably nice for you guys to have a day with no executions. No burlap jumpsuits. Nobody crying or pissing themselves. No last meals or last words. That's gotta be hard, day after day."

Elliott narrows his eyes at me as he sets my tray on my sink. "You tryin'a guilt-trip me, handsome? 'Cause I ain't fallin' for it."

"No. I just know you guys didn't exactly sign up for this," I say, repeating his drunken words from last night. "But hey, at least you won't have to do it much longer. Now that they're televising the sentencings, I'm sure you'll get some acting work soon."

Elliott steps back out of my cell and closes the door with a loud clang. He can't look at me until he wipes the flattered smirk off his face.

What a shit actor.

"When you said, 'All rise,' in the courtroom yesterday … I got chills, man. Didn't even sound like you."

Elliott purses his lips to keep from smiling as he rests a hand on the billy club hanging from his utility belt. "I'm just tryin'a shine. That's all."

"Well, good fuckin' job." I stand up and grab the tray off the sink by the door.

"Pssh." Elliott drops his eyes and waves me off, but he doesn't leave.

We're only about three feet apart now, separated by a few dozen metal bars.

"For real," I say, going in for the kill. "You know, I have some friends in the TV industry. Maybe they'll notice you tomorrow. I'm sure they'll be watching my … you know."

Elliott's face falls.

"I would offer to put in a good word for you, but I'm sure you're not allowed to let me talk to anyone. Or maybe you can. I mean … it's not like there are any laws anymore."

"Nice try, handsome, but no laws means that the chief can skin me alive and wear me like a Gucci fedora if he wants to, so ixnay on the calling your friends-ay."

I shrug. It's not like I have anyone to call anyway. I just want him to think I have something he wants.

"Why you tryin'a help me anyway? You know I can't let you go."

"I don't know, man. I've got, like, eighteen hours to live. It couldn't hurt to do somethin' nice for somebody before …"

"Before you meet your maker."

I clench my jaw and nod.

"Well, for what it's worth"—Elliott glances up at the camera at the end of the hall and turns his back to it, finishing his thought under his breath while he locks my cell—"anybody who walks the Green Mile already got themselves a one-way ticket into the pearly gates, as far as I'm concerned."

Elliott pockets his key and steps away from the bars. Using his normal volume and level of sarcasm, he says, "Eat up, buttercup. I'll be back for that tray in half an hour."

"Thanks, man," I say in a tone as low and sincere as the one he used ten seconds ago.

Then, as soon as he's gone, I shovel the gruel he brought me into my mouth in about three angry bites. I can't tell if it's oatmeal or grits or regurgitated fucking Cream of Wheat, and I don't really give a shit. I have eighteen hours to con, fight, or fucking dig my way out of here.

I'm gonna need all the energy I can get.

Rain

I DON'T KNOW HOW many times in the last few weeks that I've woken up and had no idea where I was. I've woken up in my tree house, in a tree house inside of an abandoned bookstore, on the floor in my bathroom, on the floor of an abandoned mall, in Carter's bed, and even tied up in my own garage. It usually only takes me a second or two to remember where I am and how I got there, but as I stare into the absolute darkness on this particular morning, I got nothing.

Not until I try to stretch.

My hands and feet don't get more than a foot away from my body before they're stopped by immovable walls. My eyes go wide as I reach out in front of me and hit a ceiling that's just as close. My heart begins to race, and my lungs stop working altogether as I pat and slap and thrash against the box I'm locked inside of.

I kick the roof of my prison, hearing a metallic *bang* with every blow.

Then, I hear a similar banging coming from the other side.

"Help!" I scream, kicking harder. "I'm trapped! Help!"

"Pull the handle, dumbass!" a familiar voice calls back through the steel.

Handle?

Handle!

I reach up and feel around until I find a cord with a plastic grip attached. Then, I pull it as hard as I can. The trunk lid pops open, and morning sunlight blinds me as the events of last night come back in a rush—getting a ride from the Bonys to the capitol, getting swarmed by junkies and dealers and prostitutes as soon as they left, deciding to hide in the trunk of a wrecked Dodge Charger so that I could actually get some sleep.

Guess it worked.

As I sit up and stretch my arms over my head, I groan in appreciation. My muscles feel the kind of sore that only comes from a really good night's sleep.

The gold dome of the capitol building looms over Lamar's head as a steady stream of homeless, strung-out Atlantans shuffle past us on the sidewalk. Quint fits right in as he walks over from the busted blue Toyota he spent the night in. He's been wearing the same clothes since April 23, his once-tightly-cropped hair is overgrown and matted, and for the first time in his life, he has a beard.

"Gotdamn, woman." Lamar chuckles. "It's, like, ten in the mornin'. I was about to bust in there to make sure you wasn't dead."

"Not dead yet." I yawn. "How'd you guys sleep?"

"Like shit," Quint and Lamar complain in unison.

Quint rolls his neck, careful not to stretch the side with the bandage too far, as Lamar sits down on the bumper next to me.

"Next time we decide to sleep in abandoned cars," he huffs, "I'm findin' me a Caddy or a Lincoln or somethin' with some legroom."

"Boy, you're the same height as Rain," Quint teases.

I grab my duffel bag out of the trunk and slam it shut.

"Not for long! I got them growin' pains. I'mma be taller than Carter pretty soon!"

My stomach sours at the mention of his name. I drop the bag on the trunk lid and pull out a couple of cans of soup, each one less appetizing than the one before it, but Lamar snatches the chicken and dumplings like it's made of solid gold.

"Dibs on the dumplin's!"

When the Bonys offered to give us a ride down here last night, I managed to shove all the groceries I got from Huckabee Foods into my duffel bag before climbing onto the back of a perfect stranger's dirt bike. I should have been terrified as we zigzagged through the crowded streets of Atlanta, but it just reminded me of the days I spent hugging Wes on the back of his dirt bike as we tore up the woods in Franklin Springs, looking for a bomb shelter.

Before I knew it, they were dropping us off right in front of the capitol building with nothing more than a, "Fuck 'em up, y'all," and a pat on the back.

And here we are. We've got supplies, shelter, and a means of self-defense.

If only we had a damn can opener. The one I got from home was still in Agnes's purse when it got stolen.

After scouring the abandoned cars nearby for tools and coming up empty, we end up trading a can of Mexican chicken and rice soup to an exceptionally crazy-looking homeless guy in exchange for the use of his sword.

Yeah, I said sword.

Over breakfast, the Jones brothers and I decide to start our search for Wes at the capitol building. Not for any real reason other than the fact that we are sitting right in front of it. As we walk up to the front steps, past marble life-size statues of men on horseback and toward actual, real-life men holding machine guns, I begin to get cold feet.

I stop in the middle of the cobblestone walkway and turn to face the guys.

"Uh … Rain? You okay?"

"What are we doing?" I whisper, trying to catch my breath. "The place is surrounded by cops. We can't just walk through the front door."

"First of all, we haven't done anything wrong, and second of all—"

"Look!" Lamar finishes for him, pointing at something behind me.

I lift my head and follow his gaze to a small sign posted beside the front steps.

THE GEORGIA STATE CAPITOL IS OPEN TO THE PUBLIC FOR SELF-GUIDED TOURS FROM 8 A.M. TO 5 P.M., MONDAY THROUGH FRIDAY, AND IS CLOSED ON WEEKENDS AND HOLIDAYS.

I turn back to face Quint. "I don't even know what day it is. Do you know what day it is?"

"Let's go find out." He smiles. "The worst they can do is tell us no."

"Actually, the worst they can do is shoot us in the dick," Lamar corrects.

"Boy, shut up."

I swallow my panic, along with a mouthful of saliva, and follow them up the imposing staircase to the even more imposing guards waiting for us at the top.

"Mornin', sir," Quint says to the cop blocking our entrance at the top of the stairs, cranking his Southern accent all the way up to eleven. "We've been watchin' the executions on TV and came all the way from Franklin Springs to see one in person. I noticed on your sign down there that y'all allow folks to tour the capitol. Is that right?"

The cop shares a glance with his buddy and then nods once.

"Well, ain't that a treat!" Quint slaps his knee.

"Leave all weapons and personal belongings with the officer inside before going through the metal detector. Enjoy your visit," he deadpans, eyeing my Bony sweatshirt. Then, he opens one of the heavy front doors and holds it for us.

The moment we walk over the threshold, it's like stepping through a portal into the late 1800s. The foyer is three stories high with a sweeping marble staircase right in the center. The floors are marble. The columns are marble. The statues and busts of old white men are marble. But the doors lining every wall on all three floors? Those are dark and wooden and at least eight feet tall each.

"Ma'am." A woman's voice snaps me out of my daze. "You need to check all bags, weapons, and outside food with me, please."

I stare at the female officer in disbelief. It's been so long since I've been somewhere with rules or uniforms—or employees for that matter. It's actually kind of … nice.

I tuck my gun into my duffel bag and hand it to the cop. She gives me a ticket in return and motions toward the metal detector.

We walk through and get the okay from the male officer on the other side, and as we wander aimlessly into the foyer, tears begin to blur my vision.

For the first time in months, I feel safe.

Protected.

Secure.

There are rules here.

People follow them.

No weapons allowed.

No outside food or drinks.

There are business hours.

And little yellow claim tickets.

This place has been spared from the anarchy raging outside.

And I hate how much I like it.

How good it makes me feel.

Especially when there is a twenty-five-foot-long banner hanging from the third-story railing with Governor Steele's face on it staring down at me. The quote, *There is only one true law—the law of nature*, is printed above his jowly scowl. It reminds me of the banners from the nightmares—the ones with the four horsemen of the apocalypse and the date April 23. Only this banner is even more terrifying.

Because this monster is real.

Then, I notice along the bottom of the banner, in a tidy little row, are the logos for half a dozen local businesses—Buck's Hardware. Huckabee Foods. Pizza Emporium. Lou's Liquor Superstore.

It makes me sick.

"What now, Rainy Lady?" Lamar asks.

I scan every floor, but all I see is wooden door after wooden door, the names stamped in bronze next to each one announcing which distinguished member of Congress works inside.

Or *worked* inside, I guess.

No laws probably means no congressmen. No senators. No secretaries answering phone calls.

No wonder they allow the public inside—this place is nothing more than a museum now.

"Nobody's here," I mumble as the dead eyes of every life-size portrait stare straight through me.

Nobody … including Wes.

"'Scuse me," Quint says, turning toward the officer stationed at the metal detector. "Can you point us in the direction of where the, uh, *accused* are bein' held?"

"They are in a secure, off-site location, sir."

"Off-site? Like, in another buildin'?"

"I am not at liberty to say, sir."

"Well, shoot. We was hopin' to see one up close and personal."

"Then, I suggest you come back for the Green Mile execution event tomorrow afternoon. There are spectator stands on either side of Plaza Park, but if you get a seat on the right side, the accused will walk right past you."

"Ooh, we'll do that. Thank you kindly, sir." Quint tips his invisible hat while I rush over to the desk with my yellow ticket outstretched.

I can't get out of here fast enough. Not only because the sight of Governor Steele's gaping pores makes me want to puke, but also because of what the guard just said.

Tomorrow.

We only have until tomorrow.

"Off-site," Quint repeats as we walk across the capitol building lawn, stately oaks and ancient magnolia trees shading us from the May sun.

"Oh God. Do you think they're keeping him at the jail? I assumed they were keeping the accused somewhere else because they released everybody from jail, but maybe he's there."

"Where even is the jail?" Quint asks.

"I don't ..." The words disappear on my tongue as I look across the street at a row of baby oak trees, as tidy and perfectly spaced as the list of sponsors on Governor Steele's banner.

Plaza Park looks so much smaller in real life. It's just a patch of grass in the middle of the city. Metal risers line the left and right sides, a group of police officers in riot gear laughs and drinks coffee near their patrol cars on the far side of the park, and right here in front, not much taller than the people they're now feeding on, is a row of freshly planted saplings.

I don't want to, but I find myself walking across the street, moving between the abandoned cars toward the spot where Wes's grave will be dug. The grass is perfect—just like him. Another beautiful thing that will be destroyed here tomorrow.

I kneel and run my fingers over the short green blades. I want to lie on top of them until the gravediggers come. Stop them with my body. I want to stage a protest, start a fire. But I don't know how.

I'm not that girl. I'm the one who smiles and does as she's told. I'm the one who gets good grades and doesn't start trouble. I'm the one who blends in with the bad guys instead of rising up against them.

At least, that's who I used to be. I don't even know what I am anymore. Besides desperate.

"No!" a woman shouts, which isn't anything out of the ordinary around here, except for the fact that she sounds really, really close.

"I told you, I don't have anything!"

I sit up on my knees and swing my head in all directions. Quint must be alarmed, too, because he's standing behind me with my duffel bag slung across his chest, frantically digging inside.

"Stop!" she screams. "Get off of me!" It sounds like it's coming from the direction of a black BMW with the windows broken out.

I hear a slap, followed by another scream, and before I can think better of it, I'm on my feet, darting over to Quint. I reach into the bag and find the gun tucked inside a folded pair of jeans, right where I stashed it. Quint gestures for me to give it to him, but I can't.

Because at that moment, I hear the woman growl a single word, "No."

It's long and bitter and broken and angry, but under that frustrated rage, I hear her powerlessness.

And I feel it as if it came from between my own gritted teeth.

Flipping the safety off, I sprint toward the muffled sounds of struggle—shoes scraping against asphalt, body parts thudding against the back of the car, grunting, whimpering. The noises are horrible, but they're nothing compared to the scene I find when I come around the side of the BMW. Bare skin and bare breasts and fresh blood and flailing limbs. A hand wrapped around a throat. A hand wrapped around a gun. Panties around ankles and pants around thighs. Fingernails clawing. Lips turning blue.

I want to shoot. For the first time in my life, I *want* to shoot someone. But I can't. He's too close to her.

I growl the same powerless, "No," that she did, point my gun at the sky, and fire a frustrated bullet into the air.

The greasy-haired man looks up—yellow eyes wide in surprise and yellow teeth gnashing in anger—but before he can swing his pistol in my direction, Lamar jumps out from the other side of the car, holding a whiskey bottle like a club. He bashes the sleazeball over the head so hard the bottle shatters, raining glass and the lifeless body of a possibly dead rapist down on the victim.

Quint grabs the guy's gun out of his hand as Lamar rolls his body off the traumatized woman beneath him. She's so exposed. Her skirt is bunched around her waist. Her blouse and bra are shoved up over her petite breasts. Just witnessing the emotion on her face feels like a violation, like even her soul has been bared without her consent.

"Can y'all get him out of here?" I ask, reaching for her hands to help her up.

Quint and Lamar nod and drag the scumbag away while I pull his victim to a sitting position as gently as I can. The woman cries and gasps for breath, her ruffled black hair stuck to her tears and fluttering in front of her mouth as I pull off my hoodie and drape it over her mostly naked body. She clutches it to her chest with one hand and pushes the wet strands away from her face with the other.

And now it's my turn to gasp.

The battered, bluish face in front of me belongs to Michelle Ling, the TV reporter who's been covering the executions since day one.

I kneel down beside her and place a hand on her arm. "Are you okay?"

Her chin crumples as she shakes her head. "No," she wails again, only this time, it's not angry or frustrated. There's a defeated finality to it that makes me think she's not okay for more reasons than one.

"Hey, he's gone now. Do you want to go into the capitol building? It feels safe in there."

She shakes her head again.

"Sweetie …" I don't know why I'm calling her sweetie. She's probably ten years older than me. "Do you have an office around here or a news van?"

She nods.

"Okay. Let's get you covered up, and we'll go there."

I help her adjust her clothes and pull my spray-painted hoodie on over her head. She manages to stand and pull her panties back up, wobbling on an expensive pair of red slingback heels.

They match the lipstick smeared across her face.

"Here we go," I say, wrapping an arm around her waist.

I notice Quint and Lamar standing by a dumpster about half a block away and give them a thumbs-up. I hope they threw that monster inside.

"Where to?"

Michelle points down the street, and we begin to walk.

"What were you doin' out here by yourself, honey?"

"Scouting locations." She sniffles. "I'm a reporter."

"I know who you are." I force a small smile.

Michelle hangs her head in a way that tells me she's more embarrassed about me knowing who she is than me seeing her almost naked. "There's no execution today because the governor took off to go golfing, and the station is breathing down my neck about it. They want me to get some kind of behind-the-scenes footage to show during that time slot."

She covers her face and starts to cry again. "I hate this job! I hate it!" she screams. "I hate these people!"

"Can you quit?" I ask, not knowing what else to say.

Michelle shakes her head. "I need the money." She swipes her long, thin fingers under her eyes and sniffles. "My husband died two months ago. In a car accident. I didn't find him until three days after he went missing because none of the ambulances or cops were working at that point."

"Oh my God. I'm so sorry."

"Don't be." Michelle wraps an arm around my shoulders and keeps walking. She's still shaking from the attack. "When I found him, there was a half-naked woman in the car with him, and our bank account was empty."

I shake my head. "That's so awful, Michelle. And you know what's worse? I think everybody who lived through April 23 has a story like that."

"What's yours?" she asks. Her voice sounds like an echo, like the words were formed in some hard, empty, faraway place.

I take a deep breath and try to compress my grief into as few syllables as possible. "A few days before April 23, my dad tried to kill my mom and me in our sleep with a shotgun before he turned it on himself. But I wasn't in bed like he thought."

"That is awful," Michelle mutters. No *I'm sorry*. No pity or sympathy. Just the factual observation of a jaded journalist.

It's kind of nice.

"My dad was always anxious and depressed," I continue, "a nonproductive, like the World Health Alliance lady said, but the nightmares finally made him snap. Just like they wanted them to."

Michelle shakes her head. "They're murderers. All of them. The World Health Alliance, our government leaders—they killed twenty-seven percent of the population with a few clicks of a mouse, *admitted to it*, and we're just supposed to say *thank you*?" She sounds so cold, so bitter, but her skinny arm is still wrapped around my shoulders like she needs me to keep her going. "We should be executing *them*."

The E-word makes my breath catch and my steps falter.

Michelle looks me up and down like I'm the one who needs help. "You okay?"

Leaning into her side, I nod, but then I shake my head as I inhale warm traces of vanilla on the hoodie she's wearing.

"My fiancé is supposed to be"—I have to swallow back a sob before I can say the word—"executed tomorrow."

"Oh my God. Wesson Parker? I covered his sentencing yesterday."

Michelle leads me around a corner where a sudden rotten stench slaps me in the face and makes my stomach turn on contact. Without warning, I lean over and puke on the sidewalk, right next to a dead Bony wearing a King Burger mask covered in flies.

"And I'm pregnant," I cry, wiping my mouth with the back of my hand as we stumble away from the bloated corpse. "I don't even know what I'm doing here. I don't even know where he is."

"I do," Michelle says, stopping about fifty feet short of the Channel 11 news van. Lifting a shaking finger with a jagged, broken nail clinging to the end, she points in the direction of a modern-looking building across the street.

Fulton County Police Department, the sign announces.

"He's in there."

My shoulders slump, and my heart breaks all over again as I take in the fortress in front of me.

"I'm guessing they don't have visiting hours," I mumble in complete and utter defeat.

Michelle reaches into the neck of my sweatshirt and pulls out a laminated card on the end of a lanyard. "They do if you've got one of these."

Rain

Buzz.

The exterior door unlocks after Michelle flashes her media pass at the bulletproof window. She pushes her way through with the grace of a seasoned professional despite the fact that she's wearing my spray-painted hoodie, ripped jeans, and filthy hiking boots.

The cops inside reach for their guns as soon as they see those neon-orange bones but immediately relax when the cameraman and I walk in. Or should I say, hobble in. Michelle's feet are a full size smaller than mine, so these slingback pumps are killing me.

"Good afternoon, Officers," she announces as we walk into the center of the police department lobby.

I've never been in a police station before. I expected it to feel more like a jail and less like the Department of Motor Vehicles. There is a counter where you talk to someone through a window, a few cubicles with yellowing desktop computers that look like you might have to crank 'em to start 'em up, and a sea of mismatched plastic chairs bolted to the floor.

"Officer Elliott, Officer Hoyt, this is my cameraman, Flip, and our new reporter"—Michelle looks at me with a blank expression on her face, and I freeze, realizing that I never told her my name—"Stella McCartney," she declares without missing a beat.

It's the same name that I saw printed on the label inside her skirt.

I manage to squeak out a tiny, "Hello," without letting my voice shake too much.

"Gentlemen, as you know, there will be no sentencing or execution today, so the governor has demanded that I get some behind-the-scenes coverage to show during that time slot to ensure that the one true law stays top-of-mind for the citizens of Georgia. However, as you can see"—she gestures to her outfit—"I've been involved in an … *incident.* So, Stella here is stepping in as my replacement."

The two officers—one thin, bald, and dark; the other round, shaggy, and pasty—glance at each other skeptically. They're so quiet I can hear my own heartbeat in my ears, fast and hard, before the lanky one's face splits into a grin.

"I knew it!" he yells, clapping his hands together. "I knew as soon as y'all walked in here that you were gonna interview me. Finally!" He raises his palms to the sky. "I told myself—I said, 'Marcel, you just keep doin' what you doin', baby. They gon' notice. And when they do … oooooh … you goin' to Hollywood!'" He turns to face his partner and slaps him on the arm with the back of his hand. "What did I say? What did I say?"

"Officer Elliott." Michelle clears her throat. "I'm afraid the governor has instructed us to interview the *accused*, not the staff."

The police officer's face goes somber, and that's when I recognize him.

He's the bailiff from TV.

"It would be fantastic if we could have the use of a private room with good lighting, perhaps an interrogation room or—"

"Absolutely not," a gruff voice interrupts as a man appears from the back hallway. He's older, weathered, and sporting a military haircut.

"With all due respect, Officer MacArthur, we didn't bring a lighting crew, and—"

"You will interview the inmate through the bars, and if the *governor* has a problem with the lighting situation, he can take it up with me."

"Yes, sir." Michelle nods before casting me a quick, apologetic look over her shoulder.

My heart sinks.

My palms begin to sweat.

Wes is here.

And I'm going to see him.

Through the bars.

"Very well ..." She turns to glance at Flip and me before addressing the officers again, "Shall we get started?"

Here we go.

After a quick pat-down and a trip through the metal detector, we follow all three officers through a security door and down a series of poorly lit hallways. I try to imagine how Wes must have felt while walking down these exact same passageways.

Was he scared? Was he sad? Does he miss me? Have they been mean to him?

The *click-clack* of my heels and *jingle-jangle* of the officers' tool belts echo off the tiled floor as we walk in silence. Each officer is standing next to one of us, and each one has a hand resting on his holstered weapon. We're completely unarmed—

Michelle made sure of that, knowing that we'd be searched and sent through a metal detector—so even though we're succeeding in getting closer to Wes, my hopes of breaking him out feel further and further away with every step.

Officer Elliott stops in front of an open doorway, bringing our little caravan to a halt. "Can y'all at least get a clip of me introducing the accused before you interview him?" he begs, blocking our path. "Pleeeeease?"

Michelle and Flip exchange a look.

"Uh, sure." She shrugs.

Officer Elliott's face morphs from hopeful to elated as he disappears through the doorway. "Hey, handsome! Get up! A reporter lady's here to interview you on TV, and *I* get to introduce you! And for God's sake, comb your hair or somethin'! You look a mess!"

My heart leaps into my throat when I realize who he's talking to. Who's on the other side of that doorway.

Oh my God.

It's him.

It's actually him.

He's here.

And I'm here.

How did I even get here?

It doesn't matter. I'm gonna see Wes.

And it's gonna be on TV.

Oh no.

I have to interview him.

I don't know what to say!

I don't even remember my name! McCartney? Something McCartney!

"Okay, Officer Elliott," Michelle calls out after getting the thumbs-up from her cameraman, "we're ready to roll."

Elliott appears in the doorway with the exuberance of a spokesmodel. He accepts the microphone Flip hands him and takes a deep breath, dropping into the serious bailiff character he plays on TV.

Michelle turns to me. "You ready, Stella?" she asks under her breath.

Stella! That's it!

I nod and smile through my nerves.

"Okay then. In three … two …" Flip points at Officer Elliott.

"Good afternoon, good people of Georgia. My name"—Elliott turns slightly, giving the camera his best three-quarter profile—"is Officer Marcel Elliott. I'm coming to you from a secure, undisclosed location along with reporter Stella McCartney to bring you an exclusive, behind-the-scenes interview with one of our very own *accused.* You might remember him from yesterday's sentencing. He's a heartthrob with a heart of gold. Ladies and gentlemen, I give you … Wesson … Patrick … Parker!"

Elliott steps to the side and sweeps his hand in the direction of the doorway as Michelle gives me a gentle shove from behind. I stumble three steps forward, almost rolling an ankle in her red stilettos, and look up to find one pale green eye staring at me from beneath a worried, dark brow.

And time.

Stands.

Still.

He's here.

And I'm here.

And everyone else fades away. Because a lock of shiny brown hair has fallen in front of Wes's right eye, and all I can think about is reaching through the bars and tucking it behind his ear.

Michelle clears her throat as Elliott shoves the microphone into my hand. I glance behind me at the blinking red light on top of the camera. Then, with my heart thundering in my chest and my legs as wobbly as a newborn foal's, I take another step closer to the man in the cage.

I watch his posture relax, his attitude go cool. He has no pockets to shove his hands into, so he drapes one over the crosspiece between the bars, resting his weight on his forearm.

His body is playing for the camera, for the cops, and the audience, but his face is all mine. The way he bites the inside of his bottom lip. The way the black of his pupils swallows the green. The way his Adam's apple bobs in his throat as he tries to force down his emotions.

I try to swallow mine too.

"Ms. McCartney?" Elliott prods.

Wes raises an eyebrow at me and shifts his gaze to the camera over my shoulder.

"Oh, right," I mumble to myself, looking at the microphone like it's an alien tool that I have to figure out how to operate. I tap the soft black dome with my finger before I lift it to my mouth. I tell myself to face the camera and say something, but I can't bear to pull my eyes away from the man standing in front of me.

So, I don't.

"Mr. Parker—" I clear my throat, hoping no one notices that I sound like I'm about to cry.

"Please, call me Wes."

He smiles, just for me, and the warmth I feel brings tears to my eyes.

I blink them away and try again.

"Wes"—I swallow—"how are you? I mean, in here. How are you holding up in here?"

God, I'm bombing this!

"How am I?" Wes's eyes widen in surprise. "I'm …" He shakes his head, looking for the words before a tiny smirk tugs at the corner of his mouth. "I'm better than I was a few minutes ago."

Warmth floods my cheeks as I try to come up with an actual question.

"Well … that's good. Mr. Parker—"

"Wes."

"Wes." I blush. "I saw your sentencing on TV yesterday. It was the first one ever televised. Personally, I was shocked by the lack of evidence and eyewitness testimony presented by the state as well as the lack of deliberation before you were found guilty. Do you believe you were given a fair trial?"

I exhale, relieved that I managed to ask a professional-sounding question without bursting into tears.

Wes snorts. "A fair trial? No. I was given a speaking part in *The Governor Steele Show.*"

"Had you been given a fair trial, do you think you still would have been found guilty?"

Please say no. Please say no.

"The only thing I'm guilty of is trying to help somebody I love," Wes responds, the word *love* wrapping around me like a ghost blanket.

He reaches through the bars and takes the microphone from my hand, letting his fingers graze mine in the process. The callused tips leave a trail of fire in their wake, and the moment they're gone, I have to twist the sides of my skirt in my fists to keep from reaching for him so that I can feel it again.

Wes faces the camera and gives the people of Georgia his best smolder. "I want everyone out there to picture the person they care about most. Your mother. Your child." Wes looks at me. "Your best friend. Your wife. Now, picture them injured or sick. Would you give them medicine if you thought it would save their life? Bandage their wounds? Because if so, it's just a matter of time before you're standing where I am."

I catch the sight of Michelle out of the corner of my eye, making the sign for *cut* with her hand across her throat. I guess Wes's little speech might have gone a bit too far. I reach up to take the microphone back, but he holds on to it, forcing me to stand there with my hand wrapped around his. Electricity courses through my veins as he tilts it toward my mouth so that I can speak, but I can't.

I'm touching Wes.

He's here.

He's alive.

And the only question I have left for him is one I can't ask out loud.

How do I get you out of here?

Wes

SHE'S HERE.

She's actually fucking here.

I touch her again just to make sure. I can't stop touching her.

She's so fucking beautiful—camera-ready with that slicked-back hair and red lipstick. Her big blue eyes are framed by a million jet-black lashes, but the tears welling up inside them are already starting to make her mascara run.

I want to reach up and run a thumb over her cheek, but the blinking red light on the camera five feet away keeps me from doing it. I don't know how Rain got in here or what kind of trouble she'll be facing if I blow her cover, so as much as it fucking kills me, I let go of the mic.

I let go of *her*.

"Mr. … I mean, Wes." Rain drops her eyes as a blush creeps up her neck.

I count her breaths—one, two, three—before she lifts her eyes to me again. When she does, a black tear slides down the side of her face that the camera can't see.

"You don't seem scared," she says with a worried wrinkle in her forehead.

"I'm not," I answer honestly.

"Why? Have you just … *accepted* what's gonna happen to you?" Her perfect reporter diction falters as her voice rises in frustration.

"No."

Rain straightens her spine for the camera and regains control of her Southern accent. "Then, can you tell us what's going through your mind right now?"

Her eyes plead with me to give her hope. To promise her that I have a plan. But all I have is the knowledge that I've survived every shitty fucking thing this life has thrown at me so far, and somehow, that feels like enough.

It has to be.

"Right now?" I say, staring into her eyes as if my gaze alone could dry her tears. "Right now, I'm only thinking about *right now*. About how a beautiful woman can walk into your life when you least expect it. About how quickly things can change." Rain drops her eyes again, and I can't help but smile. "And I'm also thinking of about a million and one ways I can try to escape."

Elliott snatches the microphone away from Rain with an awkward laugh and faces the camera, forcing his way in between us.

"Ha! My man Parker's got jokes, y'all! Tune in tomorrow at six to see him, and yours truly, walk the Green Mile! Stay safe out there, and may the fittest survive!"

Elliott holds his serious TV news anchor face until Flip indicates that the recording is over. Then, he lights up like a Christmas tree. "Am I a natural or what? Listen"—he steps forward and places his hands on Flip and Michelle's shoulders, turning them toward the hallway—"if y'all ever need another guest reporter, I'd be more than happy to …" His voice trails off as he walks them down the hall.

It's suddenly just me.

And Rain.

And about two-dozen steel bars in between us.

"There's a camera," I spit out before she has a chance to do or say anything incriminating.

"Don't you worry about that," Elliott's voice sings from the doorway, making Rain jump.

"Boy, when you said you had friends in the TV industry, I didn't know you meant you had *friends in the TV industry.* Haaaay!" He snaps his fingers.

"Did y'all see me? I killed that shit! I … murdered … that … shit!" Elliott claps his hands to punctuate every word. "Ooooh lawd, that felt good. Did it look good? Don't answer that. I know it looked good! Ha-*ha*!"

Rain gives me a nervous glance.

"You came through, handsome. I don't know how, but you said you was gonna help me out, and you did that shit. I'mma have me my own show in no time!"

Then, like a switch being flipped, he goes into cop mode as he turns to face Rain.

"But it's real obvious that your little friend, *Ms. McCartney,* here ain't who she says she is."

My jaw clenches shut.

No, you motherfucker. Leave her alone.

"Y'all couldn't keep ya damn hands off each other during that whole interview."

At the mention of hands, mine ball into fists.

I will fucking kill you.

"Stand-in reporter? *Please.* This bitch has about as much charisma as a mug shot. The second she walked in, I knew you two was fuckin'."

Elliott reaches into his pocket, and I try to gauge whether or not he's close enough for me to choke him through the bars.

"So I'mma do you a solid, lover boy." Elliott pulls his hand out of his pocket, producing a set of keys, and sticks one in the lock on my cell.

Then, with a wink, he yanks open the squeaky door and gives Rain a shove. Her heels click against the concrete floor as she stumbles forward, landing directly against my chest.

"Consider this your last meal." He smirks. "You got twenty minutes."

Slam!

My heart thuds in time with his footsteps as they echo down the hallway, and Rain's heart beats even faster where it's pressed against my chest.

She's here.

Holy shit.

She's right fucking here.

I wrap my arms around her trembling body and squeeze so hard I'm afraid I might crush her. Even when she's in heels, her head fits under my chin. I don't move. I don't breathe. I close my eyes and pretend that time has stopped, just for us. That tomorrow isn't coming. That we're fleshy statues now, and we can stay like this forever.

But we can't because Rain's trembles are now full-body shudders as the sob she's been trying to hold in leaks out all over my orange jumpsuit.

"Wes," she cries, burying her face in my neck. "I'm so sorry! I shouldn't have let them take you! I should have—"

"Shh." I smooth a hand over her hair and feel her breath, hot and desperate, on my skin.

Rain lifts her tear-streaked face. Her pouty red lips tremble as they pull into a frown, but before she can let out another sob, I seal her mouth with mine. She tastes sad and girlie—all salty tears and cherry lip gloss—but she kisses me back with the determination of a woman. Her tongue slides and swirls around mine. Her tits, practically bursting out of that too-tight blouse, press against my chest. And her hands dive into my hair, holding me like a balloon in danger of floating away. Then, her kisses begin to roam.

"I love you so much," she murmurs, kissing my cheek.

"Oh my God, I missed you." Her kisses trace the line of my jaw.

"This is all my fault." She breathes against my neck. "I'm gonna get you out. I promise. I'll … I'll figure something out."

"Hey." I capture her face in my hands and tilt it back so that I can stare directly into her wide, panicking eyes when I tell her, "I'll get myself out. Do you hear me? You shouldn't be here."

Rain's eyelids close as she exhales a quiet, shuddering sob. "This is the only place I want to be."

Without looking up, Rain grips my zipper and slides it down my chest. I grit my teeth as she reaches in and wraps her arms around my exposed torso, pressing her wet cheek against my bare skin. My eyes sting. My lungs scream for air. Nothing fucking hurts as much as this woman's touch. It filets me like a dull knife. At first, it hurt because I realized that no one had ever cared for me like that before. Then, it killed me because I knew once she left, no one ever would again. But now? Now, her love cuts me down where I stand because I can no longer deny how much I want it.

I don't want to die for her or let her go or try to convince myself that she belongs with someone else. I never did. The soul-crushing truth is that I want her more than I've ever wanted anything. I want her by my side and in my bed and in my life forever. I still don't believe that God will let me have her, but until he pries her out of my cold, dead hands, I'm going to keep fighting.

Rain pushes the orange fabric over my shoulders, and I shrug it off like a skin I've outgrown. Her fingernails graze my sides as she kisses my tattoos, lingering over the wilted pink lily on my ribs. My fist grips her hair as her fingertips trace the edge of my government-issued boxers. Rain slides them down slowly as she sinks to her knees. I can feel my heartbeat in my cock as it falls forward, seeking her warmth. As badly as I want to yank her back up and fuck her properly, the image of her red lips wrapped around my dick is one I simply can't go to my grave without seeing.

Rain's black lashes fan out across her flushed cheeks as she licks me from base to tip, swirling her tongue around my swollen, throbbing head. My chest aches as she takes me into her mouth, as I watch her crimson lips slide over my cock and her cheeks hollow as she sucks me off, but when she opens her big blue eyes and looks up at me, the sensation is more intense than I ever fucking imagined.

This is her love for me. This is her selflessness. This is her risking her life to get to me, just to spend what little time we have left trying to make me feel good.

"Come here," I whisper, cupping her face and wiping the mascara from under her eyes with my thumbs.

Rain doesn't break eye contact as she slides her lips down my length one last time, and I'm overwhelmed with the need to feel her everywhere. I pull her to her feet and make quick work of the buttons on her blouse as I nip and suck at the overheated skin beneath her ear.

"We don't have much time left, and I want to spend it inside you," I growl, feeling a ripple of goose bumps pebble under my lips.

Yanking her tight skirt up over her full hips, I palm her perfect, round ass as I kiss my way down to her bra. Sucking one straining nipple through the black lacy fabric, I slide my hand between her legs and tease her slit over her panties. They're already soaked through. My mouth waters. I know we don't have much time left, but I need to lick her. I need to taste her.

If this is my last meal, I'm gonna fucking savor it.

Dropping to my knees, I trace the edge of Rain's silky panties with my finger before sliding them to one side. I don't take my time, and I don't ease her in. I run my tongue along her soft, slippery flesh and stifle a moan as the flavor coats my tongue.

Fucking perfect.

Rain hisses and grabs my hair as I suck and lick and devour her pussy, alternating between pulling me closer and trying to push me away.

"Wes," she whispers, her voice needy and breathless. "Please. I need you."

Those words are my undoing. I press her back against the one cinder-block wall that's hidden from the hallway, pull her knee over my hip, and fill her so deep and so hard that she has to bite my lip to keep from moaning.

"Fuck," I snarl, filling her again.

She feels so fucking good, so warm and soft and right and *mine*, that for a minute, I wonder if I'm already dead.

Not even heaven could feel as good as this.

"I love you," Rain whispers against my mouth.

The sadness in her shaky voice hits me like a fist to the heart.

I wrap my hand around her jaw and force her to look at me as I thrust into her again. "I love you more."

It's not a fucking question.

"If I can't get you out of here …" Her words trail off with a gasp.

"That's not your job. Do you hear me? You just stay safe."

Rain closes her eyes, and I feel her chin buckle under my palm. "I can't lose you, Wes."

"Hey, look at me."

Rain opens her tortured eyes and slays me with a single sentence. "*We* can't lose you."

We.

I gaze down the length of her beautiful torso, over her swollen, flushed-pink tits, and down to her still-flat belly. I realize I'm no longer fucking her.

I'm marveling at her.

"I took a test." She swallows. "You were right."

"Fuck. Rain …" I cup her face in my hand and kiss her again, not out of lust or loss or the elapsing of time, but out of pure, soul-crushing love.

When I fill her again, it's because that's the only way I can get closer to her. And when I feel her contract around me, when her breaths turn to whimpers and she whispers that she loves me again, I pour myself into her on a muffled cry.

I thought I wanted to be a good dad, like Doug.

But fuck that.

Good dads die for their families.

I'm gonna live for mine.

Rain

I STAND IN THE center of Wes's cell with my arms wrapped around his waist and my cheek pressed against his chest, waiting, counting his heartbeats until the next horrible thing happens.

Eighteen ... *nineteen* ... *twenty* ...

"Remember what I said," Wes whispers into my hair.

I nod, feeling my own heart beating about twice as fast as his. I tighten my fist around my balled-up panties. Any second now, that door is going to open, and Wes is going to attack Officer Elliott. As soon as Wes has his arms pinned behind his back, my job is to strangle Officer Elliott until he passes out. Wes said it might be too hard for me to do with my bare hands, so I should wrap my panties around his neck and tighten them instead.

I can't believe we're about to do this.

The calming thump of Wes's heartbeat is suddenly drowned out by the panic-inducing clomp of hard-sole shoes coming down the hall.

I squeeze my eyes shut and cling to him tighter.

"Okay, lovebirds," Elliott sings from the hallway behind me as his footsteps come to a stop. "Time's up."

I feel Wes bristle in my arms, so I look over my shoulder at the man on the other side of the bars. Officer Elliott has a huge grin on his face … and a small handgun in his fist.

"Ms. McCartney, you come on over here, hon." He gestures to the door with the barrel of the gun. "Handsome, you go stand in the corner with ya hands up."

And just like that, our escape plan is ruined. Wes can't jump Elliott if he's got a gun pointed at him at point-blank range.

And we all know it.

"Fuck," Wes hisses, squeezing me tighter.

"Shh … it's okay," I whisper, tilting my head back to look at him. His nostrils flare with every breath. "I'll see you tomorrow, okay?"

I don't even know why I said that. Maybe because it's the closest thing to goodbye I can bring myself to say, or maybe it's because it's true. One way or another, I'm gonna see him tomorrow. Either in my arms after I rescue him or in Plaza Park when I lose him forever.

"Tomorrow? Oh my goodness, are you goin' to the Green Mile event?" Officer Elliott asks enthusiastically. "Ooh! Maybe you could talk to Michelle Ling for me! See if I can introduce *the governor* this time!"

"Yeah, okay," I mumble, not taking my eyes off Wes's beautiful, tortured face. "Tomorrow," I promise again, pushing up onto my toes to kiss his tightly drawn lips.

"Tomorrow," Wes growls before his mouth crashes into mine, finally letting every ounce of the panicked desperation he's been feeling make itself known.

My back arches as I try to absorb the brunt of his brutal kiss, the feral force of his love, the overwhelming power of his will to survive. I feel Wes becoming a caged animal in my arms, and my heart breaks, both for him and for anyone in this building who makes the mistake of coming too close to him.

Clang! Clang! Clang!

Officer Elliott taps his gun against the bars. "You got three seconds to get in the corner with your hands up before I shoot, boy. Don't make me hafta drag yo' dead ass down the Green Mile tomorrow!"

I break our kiss and wriggle out of Wes's death grip, walking him backward into the corner of his cell.

"I love you," I whisper, holding him at arm's length.

A lock of hair falls over one pale green eye as he stares down at me. Unbridled rage swims in the other. "Tomorrow," he grinds out through clenched teeth.

I force a smile through my tears and nod. "Tomorrow."

Tearing myself away from him and tearing my own heart out in the process, I turn and take three steps over to the bars.

Officer Elliott unlocks the door and yanks me out without once taking his eyes off of Wes. As soon as the door slams shut, he turns to me and beams. "So, here's my vision. Instead of Michelle doing her usual boring-as-hell intro, what if the camera follows *me*, leading the accused all the way down the Green Mile? Make folks feel like they're really there!"

As he walks me away, with a grin on his face and a gun pressed between my shoulder blades, I glance over my shoulder.

I used to love nothing more than watching Wes watch me. His rapt attention. His intense gaze. With a single look, he could make me feel seen. Studied. Special.

But watching him watch me go is an entirely different experience. I don't feel special.

I feel split apart.

Officer Elliott rambles the entire way back to the lobby about all his TV show ideas, but I'm not listening. I'm too busy trying to remember how to breathe. Just before he buzzes us into the lobby, he holsters his gun and starts laughing like we're old friends.

"Y'all come on back anytime, Ms. McCartney," he says, giving me a little shove.

Officer Hoyt looks up from the front desk but drops his gaze the moment our eyes meet.

"Thank you, Officer Elliott," I mumble without turning around. And I'm surprised to realize that I mean it.

I really hope Wes doesn't kill you.

"Thank *you*, honey child. And be sure to tell ya boy Flip to get my good side tomorrow!"

"Which side is your good side?" Officer Hoyt asks as I click-clack over to the main entrance, trying to hold my head up and my sobs in.

"Both sides, silly!" Officer Elliott howls with laughter as the door buzzes open.

I walk outside and squint into the daylight.

The world before me looks just as abused and miserable and desperate and filthy as I feel.

But the sun is still shining.

Wes is still alive.

And the Channel 11 news van is still waiting for me out front.

And for that, I'm grateful.

As I drag my grieving bones across the street to the Channel 11 news van, the passenger door opens, and Michelle climbs out.

"You okay?" she asks, her battered face mirroring my battered spirit.

I nod. Then shrug. Then shake my head as she comes over to give me a hug.

"If it makes you feel any better, I think this footage is gonna have everybody in Georgia on Team Wes as soon as it airs. He's a hottie, huh?" Michelle forces a smile as she tugs me closer to the van.

Opening the side doors, she gestures for me to climb inside. Flip is in the driver's seat while Quint and Lamar are sitting in two small fold-out chairs. The three of them are chowing down on soup straight out of the can. A skinny counter wraps around the back and driver's side of the van, and above it are rows of monitors, lights, switches, and buttons.

Lamar greets me with a grin. "Hey, Rainy Lady!"

"How'd it go?" Quint asks, setting his can on the counter.

I sit in the middle of the floor and try to pry off one of Michelle's cruel shoes. It's so tight on my foot that I end up yanking it off with both hands and throwing it across the van. "Ugh!"

"So … not good?" Lamar summarizes.

I screw my eyes shut and shove my hands into my hair, tugging as hard as I can to distract myself from the pain. A squeal emanates from somewhere deep inside of me, high and pained and pressured, like a teakettle about to blow.

"What the hell happened?" Michelle asks, climbing in behind me and shutting the doors. "You were in there for, like, half an hour!"

"I had him!" I shout, hot, angry tears leaking through my closed eyelids. "I had him, and I fucking lost him!" I take a few deep breaths and try to calm down. Try to force my brain to think.

Think, Rain. Keep it together.

"He's right there!" I growl, shoving my hand in the direction of the police station. "He's right here, and I can't get him out!"

"What happened in there?" Michelle repeats her question as she climbs back into the passenger seat.

I suck in another deep breath and cover my mouth with my hands. "They have guns. That's what happened."

"We have guns," Quint offers.

"We have two guns." I snort.

Flip lifts his pant leg, revealing a small silver pistol in an ankle holster.

"Okay, three guns. Even if we managed to take out the cops in the lobby without getting shot, there are probably more officers inside. All they'd have to do is seal the doors, and then we'd be sitting ducks."

Michelle shakes her head. "This whole Green Mile operation is run by, what … the governor, a handful of police officers at the station, maybe a dozen riot cops, and a couple of security guards at the capitol? What is that, like, twenty people?"

"If we could just get the Bonys on our side, we'd have enough people to fight back or even the runaways from the mall." Lamar raises his voice in excitement. "Q is fuckin' crazy. I bet she'd kill a cop."

I sigh. "I tried to get her to come, but you know her. Q only does what's good for Q."

"You know who would probably love to help? All those prisoners they just released," Quint suggests. "Nobody hates cops more than criminals, right?"

"There's enough guns in this country to arm every man, woman, and child," Flip mumbles around a mouthful of loaded potato soup. "All you need is, like, a hundred of 'em."

My shoulders slump. "How do we even find that many people? Look around. Everybody's just tryin'a survive. They're not gonna put their necks on the line for people they don't know."

"Damn." Michelle's mouth draws into a frown as she reaches for a bottle of vodka next to a monitor. "I wish we could broadcast a message for you, but they'd kill us as soon as they saw it."

I stare into the black monitor next to her as she takes a long pull from the bottle, seeing only my reflection staring back at me.

Broadcast.

Message.

As soon as they saw it.

"What if they don't see it?" I blurt out, my eyes darting back to Michelle's. "What if we fight fire with fire?"

"What are you talkin' about?" Flip asks as Michelle chokes on her last swallow of vodka.

"I'm talking about subliminal messaging! That's how they programmed us to think the world was gonna end, right? How they drove a quarter of us insane enough to kill ourselves or get ourselves killed. What if we do the exact same thing *against* them? We could plant a subliminal message in the interview footage that makes people want to fight back!"

Michelle shakes her head. "Stella …"

"My name is Rain."

"Rain … we only have a few hours to get back to the newsroom and upload that interview. Where are we gonna find that kind of content? Or software even?" Michelle turns to Flip. "Can our programs even splice images in at intervals that small?"

Flip shrugs as Quint gestures to the computer screens. "Can't you just find the images online?"

Michelle's mouth falls open. "Have you guys not been online since April 23?"

We shake our heads in unison.

Michelle huffs in exasperation. "It's unusable! With no laws, it's been completely overrun by hackers. If you go online through anything other than a secure government server, you'll have your identity stolen, your bank account emptied, and you'll be locked out of your device in seconds."

I groan and fall back in my chair, rubbing my eyes with both hands. "So, where do we find a secure server?"

"Well, they have one at the TV station, but I am *not* working on this there." Michelle takes another gulp from her bottle before passing it to Flip.

He accepts it with a polite nod and turns to face me. "Pretty much any government buildin' should have a secure server. You just gotta be able to get inside and plug in."

My eyes drift over to the heavily tinted windows on the side of the van. Just beyond them, rising like both a beacon of hope and symbol of death, is the glowing gold dome of the capitol building.

"Michelle"—I swallow—"you still got that media pass?"

Wes

ONCE, WHEN I WAS, like, eight, I went on a school field trip to the zoo. My mom was too fucked up on whatever her drug of choice was at the time to sign the permission slip, but my teacher must have forged that shit because, when the day came, they let me get on the bus right along with everybody else.

I'd never been to the zoo before. Hell, I'd never been on a field trip before. I was so fucking excited, but once we got there, all I felt was sad. These big, magical beasts—creatures I'd only ever seen on TV—were locked up in cages like criminals. They hardly moved. They ignored us completely. Even the lions, the kings of the fucking jungle, were just lying on rocks, waiting to die. Every motherfucker there had accepted their fate.

Except the fucking tiger.

The tiger was the only animal there who was in solitary confinement. And he was the only animal there who was pacing. Not lazy, *I'm just gonna stretch my legs* pacing, but fucking-head-down, eyes-on-the-prize, *I'm gonna find a way out of this motherfucker* pacing. He would do a lap around the perimeter of his cage, pushing on the Plexiglas walls with his body. Then, he would do figure eights around all the trees, which had been cut short to keep him from climbing out.

There was something different about him. Something that made him refuse to accept his circumstances, like the others. And now, I know what it was.

Somewhere out there, that motherfucker had a mate.

I could live in here quite fucking comfortably if Rain were locked up too. We could fuck and talk and feed each other and make fun of Elliott all goddamn day. But without her, I feel like that fucking tiger. I want to climb the walls. I want to scrape the mortar out from in between the cinder blocks with my bare hands. I want to rip the face off the next piece of shit who rattles my bars.

But unlike that tiger, I *am* gonna get the fuck out of here.

Because unlike that tiger, I'm not gonna let them know I'm restless.

If he had acted as lazy as the lions, those zookeepers might have gotten lazy too. Maybe let his trees grow a little too long. Maybe used a little less caution when they opened the door to feed him. An opportunity would have presented itself.

Which is exactly why I'm lying on my cot, staring at the ceiling, trying to act bored, when all I want to do is punch holes in the walls and wear a figure eight into the floor with my pacing.

Clomp. Clomp. Clomp.

Hard-sole shoes approach, but they're not the spirited footsteps of Officer Elliott. Nor are they the slow shuffles of Officer Hoyt. No, these punishing footsteps belong to someone angrier. Someone who must be picturing the faces of his mortal enemies on every unpolished floor tile. Someone with a gray buzz cut and a burgeoning beer gut.

Officer MacArthur appears outside my door with a scowl on his leathery face and the scent of cheap whiskey emanating from his pores.

"Parker," he snaps, addressing me like I'm one of his soldiers.

But I don't fucking salute.

"That's me," I deadpan, tucking my hands behind my head.

"I'm here to take you to the showers. The governor insists on the accused looking decent for the Green Mile."

"Did you pull the short straw or somethin'?" I ask. "Why isn't Elliott or Hoyt takin' me?"

"That's Officer Elliott and Officer Hoyt to you, son," he growls. "And I'll be taking you because the accused tend to get a little aggressive at this point in their sentence."

"Ah," I say, sitting up with a stretch. "So you're the muscle, huh?"

"Step over to the door and place your hands through the bars."

I do as he said, my movements as slow and despondent as a caged lion's.

He clamps a pair of handcuffs around my wrists as tight as they'll go before saying, "Now, stick your feet out, one at a time."

I do that, too, watching for signs of intimidation or fear. He's not shaking, not nervous. But he's shackling me just as tightly as he cuffed me, which tells me I haven't fully convinced him of my apathy.

I wait for him to unlock my door and marvel at how clear-eyed he seems for somebody who smells like the bottom of a bottle of Jim Beam.

"You former military?" I ask as he guides me by the bicep into the hall.

He grumbles in response but eventually spits out, "Army. Special Forces."

"No shit? That's pretty badass, man. Were you, like, a paratrooper or something?"

"Sniper," he mutters under his breath.

Sniper. My fists flex, and blood surges to my extremities. *There's only one thing they need a sniper for around here.*

We walk past an open office door, and the image of my own face stops me in my tracks. There's a monitor above the desk broadcasting the interview Rain did earlier. I watch myself lean against the bars, orange polyester from the neck down, poorly masked shock and awe from the neck up. The back of Rain's head and a sliver of the side of her face are visible on the screen. I want to reach out and run my fingers through her slicked-back black hair as she stutters and stumbles over her first question to me.

"Mr. Parker—"

"Please, call me Wes."

"Wes ... how are you? I mean, in here. How are you holding up in here?"

My throat tightens at the sound of her shaky voice. On camera, she looks fucking amazing, but from where I was standing, she was all teary eyes and trembling hands.

And red fucking lips.

"How am I? I'm ... I'm better than I was a few minutes ago."

Mac coughs out a laugh and claps me on the shoulder. "Pretty smooth, boy. That replacement they got for Michelle Ling was a stone-cold fox, wasn't she?" He tugs me by the arm down the hall, coughing and chuckling and coughing some more.

I grind my teeth and try to concentrate on keeping my breathing even. I want to put my fist through the guy's face, but I can't let him see me sweat.

I try to figure out an angle as we turn down the next hallway and stop in front of the cabinet where they keep the soap and towels. I can't play on his guilty conscience like Hoyt because this dude is literally a trained killer. I can't play to his vanity like Elliott because … fucking look at him. But maybe, since he's a military guy, I can appeal to his sense of justice. Make him see that what they're doing here is wrong.

That what *he's* doing is wrong.

"Michelle Ling looked pretty roughed up, huh? I wonder what happened to her."

"Probably got jumped by a meth-head or a Bony." Mac shrugs, pulling a towel out of the cabinet and draping it over his arm.

"That has to be hard for a guy like you … seeing all that crime happening right outside your door and not being able to do anything about it."

Mac grabs a nondescript white bottle, which I assume has some kind of shampoo in it, and closes the cabinet. "It's not a crime if it's legal," he mutters, but there's no conviction in his voice. It sounds rehearsed, like it's just something he tells himself so he can sleep at night.

Mac pulls open the shower room door without looking at me, and I walk in without being asked.

After setting the towel on a hook next to one of the open shower stalls, Mac puts the shampoo bottle on a shelf inside and turns on the faucet. The pipes are rusty and exposed, and they rattle and hiss louder than an oncoming earthquake.

Good.

"Just because it's legal doesn't make it *right*," I say as Mac bends down to take off my shackles. "Attacking an innocent woman? Robbery? Rape? Isn't that why you got into this job in the first place? To protect the good guys and punish the bad guys?"

"I don't make the rules," Mac snaps, obviously annoyed with my line of questioning. "I just enforce 'em."

The shackles clatter to the ground as Mac stands, pressing a hand to the small of his back as his knees and random other joints snap, crackle, and pop.

"That's apparent." I snort, holding my wrists out for him to uncuff next. "The bad guys are literally getting away with murder while you're busy shooting good guys in the head on live TV."

Mac's eyes slam up to mine the moment the second cuff falls free.

"Yeah, I know you're the executioner. I figured it out as soon as you said you were a sniper. But it's cool, man. You're just doing what you gotta do, right?" I unzip my jumpsuit, pausing when I get to the sharpened toothbrush stashed in the waistband of my boxers. "And so am I."

Grabbing the shiv, I catch Mac completely off guard as I plunge it into the side of his neck, using my left arm to block him from going for his gun. He yells in pain, but the thumps and rattles and hissing and splashing from the shower muffle his cry.

Mac goes for his gun with his left hand as I struggle with his right, but the awkward cross-body reach doesn't allow him to flip the snap to unlock the weapon from his holster. Doing some kind of spin move, he twists out of my hold, but I grab his billy club and duck the second he gets a hand on his gun. When Mac spins around to shoot, I bash him in the kneecap with it, sending him to the floor. I grab the hand holding the gun on his way down and try to pry his fingers off by pulling his trigger finger back as far as it will go. He yells in pain and punches me in the side of the head with his free hand. Repeatedly. I feel his arthritic knuckles crunch against my skull. I shift my weight and curl around the hand holding the gun so that he can only punch me in the back now. Then, I bite his thumb *and* pull backward on his finger as hard as I fucking can until the gun falls free. We both scramble for it, sending it sliding across the tile floor.

"Shit," I hiss right before Mac rears back and clocks me right in the jaw.

I see spots as I reach into the shower for the dropped billy club and crack him over the head with it. Instead of knocking him out, Mac's eyes glaze over with rage, and he attacks me with everything he's got.

Fists rain down on me as I back up into the scalding hot spray of the shower. I try to block his swings with one hand while using the other one to swing and stab at him with the club. I can't connect with anything other than his sides and shoulders, so I change tactics and shove the club up under his chin, pushing until he can't breathe and is forced to let go of me. The second he does, we both scramble for the gun again, and again it turns into a bloodbath. My ribs crack under his fists. His nose breaks against my palm. My elbow drops into his gut. His knee comes up to meet mine. What I have on Mac by way of youth and agility, he more than makes up for with skill. We are nothing but sopping wet fists and teeth and adrenaline and fear. But I have something Mac doesn't have.

A damn good reason to live.

My lungs burn and my eyes burn and my entire fucking body feels like it's been pulverized by a meat grinder as we wrestle under the searing hot water, but it's not quite as bad as I let on. See, I might not be able to use Mac's guilt or his vanity or even his sense of justice to get what I want, but he's got something even easier to exploit.

Pride.

Good thing I got that shit beat out of me by the eighth grade.

Leaving myself open to a few blows that feel like sledgehammers, I let Mac think he has the upper hand. I can almost see his ego swell as he lands a solid right cross to the cheekbone of the punk twenty-two-year-old who dared to take on the legendary Officer MacArthur. And I can almost hear it shatter into a million pieces when he rears back to clock me again and feels a solid steel cuff click into place around his wrist.

Scurrying backward out of the shower on my elbows, I watch as Mac's eyes go wide in horror. He sits up on his haunches and thrashes in place as he realizes that I've handcuffed him to the shower pipe.

I reach the gun across the room just as he reaches for his taser, but when he holds it up, it's dripping wet and completely worthless.

The look on his face as he drops the taser and raises his hands in the air is something I'll never forget as long as I live. I've seen it on TV a few times now but never in person. Never staring down the barrel of my own gun.

It's the look of a man who knows he's about to die.

His nose is gushing blood, which the shower dilutes into a pink stream that courses over his swollen mouth and down his neck. His chest is heaving even harder than mine, but his hands aren't shaking nearly as bad.

"You fought well, son." He spits through the bloody water.

"So did you, old man." I close one eye and aim for his forehead. "Between the eyes, right? That's your style?"

He nods without remorse. "Instant kill."

His words send a shiver down my wet, bruised spine as I tighten my finger around the trigger.

But I'm not like Mac.

I'm not a cold-blooded killer.

Which is exactly why the fuck I need him.

Rain

“YOU GOT IT UPLOADED and everything?” I whisper as Flip closes his laptop.

“Uploaded. Broadcasted. It’s done.” He looks over at me, the blue digital glow from the servers illuminating his tired face.

“Oh my God.” I cover my mouth with my hoodie sleeves.

“And you got all the images in there without them being too obvious?” Michelle asks, rubbing her exposed arms to stay warm. They must keep the air-conditioning on full blast in here to cool off all the equipment.

“Yes, ma’am.” Flip stands up and stretches. “Folks are gonna have some real wild dreams tonight.”

I launch myself at him and wrap my arms around his middle. "Thank you. Thank you so much. You have no idea …" I ramble as Flip awkwardly pats me on the back.

"I hope it works, hon. Now, if you don't mind, I'd like to get the hell outta here before nightfall."

Michelle stands up and smooths her hands over her black pencil skirt, which I can see now is actually a little loose on her. She's probably lost weight since she bought it from all the stress.

I let go of Flip and attack her with my gratitude next.

Hugging me right back, Michelle says, "You gonna be okay tonight? If you need a place to stay …"

"I'll be all right. I wanna stay nearby in case something happens."

What I mean is, *I'm going to spend the night locked in the trunk of a car outside the police station, praying that my boyfriend escapes before they execute him.*

I look over at the Jones brothers, who are sitting against a shelving unit full of servers on the other side of the room. Their eyes are closed, and their heads are propped against one another's.

"Y'all go ahead," I say, nodding toward my sleeping friends. "I seriously can't thank you enough."

"You sure?" Michelle asks, holding me at arm's length.

I nod. "I'm sure. I'll see you tomorrow." Those words remind me of the last person I said that to just a few hours ago. The place where my heart used to be aches in response.

"Yes, you will." She smiles, but it looks all wrong on her.

As Michelle and Flip tiptoe out of the capitol's server room, I walk over to Quint and gently shake his shoulder.

"Wake up, guys. It's done. Time to go."

"Hmm?" Quint smacks his lips without opening his eyes.

"We gotta go. We've been in here for, like, two hours. The guards are probably already lookin' for us."

Lamar sits up with a yawn. "Did you do it?"

"I think so. Come on!"

The boys grumble but slowly pull themselves to their feet.

I grab my duffel bag off the floor and toss it over my shoulder before pressing my ear to the door. When I don't hear anything, I open it just a crack.

"You get what you need, Ms. Ling?" The voice of the male security guard echoes through the rotunda.

"Yes, thank you. There was no way we could have made it to the station to upload our footage in time with the roads being the way they are," Michelle replies with her patented, matter-of-fact reporter voice.

"Happy to help."

"That was a great interview, by the way," the female guard adds.

"Thank you. My stand-in, Ms. McCartney, will be along shortly. She just had to … use the restroom."

"I think we're good," I whisper to Quint and Lamar as I open the second-story door and tiptoe out into the wide hallway.

There's significantly less light coming in from the windows in the main entryway than when we got here, increasing my sense of urgency.

I've seen this place at night. If we want to live to see morning, we need to find a place to hide before dark.

We should be talking, I think as we near the end of the hall. *We're being too quiet. They're gonna know something's up.*

I turn to say something to Quint, *anything*, but the words shrivel up and die in my mouth when I notice that his brother is no longer following us.

I swing my head in all directions and find him just before he disappears through a door.

A massive wooden door with the words *Office of the Governor* painted on the frosted-glass window in white and gold letters.

"Lamar!" I whisper.

"Shit!" Quint hisses.

We follow him as quietly as possible but freeze when voices ring out from the atrium behind us.

"Governor! We didn't expect you back until tomorrow morning. How was your outing?"

"Pretty damn good, Officuh. Pretty damn good. I suspect those old bastards let me win, but a win's a win in my book."

"Spoken like a true politician," a third voice that I don't recognize jokes, causing everyone to laugh.

Quint and I glance at each other in horror and dash inside the governor's office to grab Lamar. The lights are on inside, illuminating what looks like a time capsule from the 1900s. The front room must be a lobby. It's filled with heavy wooden furniture upholstered in navy blues and deep reds, regal-looking carpet, brass light fixtures, and oil paintings of ducks and dogs and old white men.

Through the open door across from the entrance is Governor Steele's office. His land yacht of a wooden desk is parked in the back, in front of a navy-blue curtain with the golden seal of Georgia in the center. But I'm more interested in the person standing in front of his desk, relieving himself all over Governor Steele's rug.

"Lamar! What the hell you doin'?" Quint snaps as I shield my eyes. "We gotta go! Now!"

"I just needed to stop by the little boy's room on the way," Lamar says with a chuckle.

"Well, put your pecker away, and let's go! Are you fuckin' crazy?"

I hear the zip of Lamar's fly and lower my hand.

"Calm down. I was just leavin' a little surprise for this asshole to find when he gets back from his—"

Lamar's eyes go wide as we hear the creak of the main door. He bolts, diving behind the governor's desk, as Quint and I duck behind a pair of leather wing chairs.

"Tell the SWAT team I'm gonna hafta move the execution to tomorrow mornin'. I've got a meetin' with Tim Hollis in the aftuhnoon to discuss some *sponsuhship* opportunities," a familiar old-South accent announces as he walks into the lobby.

"The CEO of Burger Palace?" the other male voice I heard in the atrium asks.

"The one and only. Good man. Shit golfuh." The governor chuckles as they walk through the door into the main office. "I convinced that son-of-a-bitch to pay five billion dolluhs to be the official sponsuh of the Green Mile execution event!"

"No fucking way."

"Yes, suh! That's why I need that hundred-year-old bottle of scotch. You and I gon' celebrate tonight! We're gonna rename Plaza Park *Burger Palace Park* and use drones to film the executions from all angles. We'll have aerial shots of the bodies fallin' in the holes. It's gonna be glorious."

My stomach turns, and my palms get so sweaty one of them slides off the leather chair, causing me to almost lose my balance. Quint glares at me in warning.

"You'll get national coverage for sure," the other man says.

I can see him now as they walk right through the wet spot that Lamar left on the rug. He's dressed in all black, like a bodyguard.

The governor clicks his tongue and shoots a finger gun at the man. "Bingo. The only thing left to figyuh out is whether it'll be bettuh to paint King Burger on the lawn or use a projector to make him all animated-like."

"I think the real question is, where are you gonna hang all your deer heads once you move into the White House?"

Governor Steele chuckles as he comes around the side of the desk. "Once *we* move into the White House. I'm gonna make you head of the Secret Service, my friend."

I reach out and grab Quint's arm, the ghost of my heart slamming against my ribs as the governor opens his top drawer and takes out a bottle of liquor. Shutting it, he looks down at his overstuffed chair with a frown.

"Now, why in the hell is my chair pulled out?"

"Hey, Beau?" his security guy asks, pulling a gun from his side holster. "You didn't leave your lights on last night when you left, did you?"

I clutch Quint's arm tighter as the governor's bodyguard pushes him out of the way and points the barrel of his gun at the cavernous opening under his desk.

Please don't let them find him, I pray. *Please, God. He's just a kid. Please, please, please don't let them—*

Suddenly, I feel a kiss on my cheek, so quick I think I might have imagined it, before the arm that I was clutching slips out of my grasp. I look up from my crouched position and reach for Quint, but my fingers grasp nothing but the last breath he exhaled before he disappeared around the front of his chair.

No! Quint!

"Death to sheep!" he cries, running for the door.

And then there's a bang so loud I almost scream.

And a thump.

And a deep, guttural groan.

I clutch the chair for support and hold in my cries as Quint slaps at the floor, trying to drag himself into the lobby.

"What in the hell?" the governor shouts, clutching his chest.

"Goddamn it, Beau! I told you we gotta stop allowing tours!"

I bite my lip as their footsteps approach and screw my burning eyes shut as the men stand beside my oldest friend.

BLAM!

Then … nothing.

"Nice job, Jenkins. You really were Special Forces, huh?"

"Green Berets, sir."

Governor Steele slaps him on the back. "Come on. Now, I really need a drink. I'll have Edna and the cleaning crew take care of that."

The two men leave as I cling to the chair like it's a loved one, silently crying into the Italian leather, my fingers wedged between the brass rivets.

But it doesn't hold me back.

My face contorts against the wet hide as pain slices me from ear to ear, stretching my mouth in a wordless scream.

Loss.

Loss.

Loss.

Loss.

Every week, every day, another one. No matter what I do, no matter how hard I try to save them, I can't.

Powerless.

Weak.

Worthless.

Stupid.

And now, Wes is going to be executed tomorrow for saving the life of someone who died anyway.

Pointless.

Meaningless.

Hopeless.

Death.

Slowly, the sound of agony, high-pitched and constant, breaks through the fog of silence in the room. It feels like mine. Sharp. Brittle. Unending. Unrelenting.

But it's coming from under the desk.

I want to go to him. Hold him like a mother. Shush him and tell him it's going to be all right.

But I can't.

Because it's not.

And it never will be again.

"Get up," I bark, standing from my hiding spot.

Quint's body is laid out in the middle of the doorway between the lobby and the office, a maroon blanket covering his back and seeping into the carpet all around him.

Lamar sniffles, but then he begins sobbing even louder.

He always does this. He gets in trouble, and then Quint takes the punishment. How many times did Quint get a whooping from their drunk old man for something that Lamar had done, and how many more times did Lamar get in trouble, knowing Quint would show up just in time to take the fall?

Selfish.

Spoiled.

Ungrateful.

Brat.

Stomping over the desk, I pull the chair out even further, prepared to scream at Lamar—to unleash the pain and rage and helplessness and injustice bottled up inside of me—but the boy I find huddled under there, hugging his knees and weeping into his elbows, looks so much like his brother at that age that I slump to the floor and crawl inside with him.

Wrapping my arms around Lamar's shuddering body, I realize how small he still is. How young.

"Shh," I whisper, rocking him back and forth. "Shh …"

"I killed him," Lamar whispers back. "I killed him, Rain."

"No," I choke out, his short, unkempt dreadlocks soaking up my tears. "*They* killed him, baby. They kill everybody. It doesn't matter what you do." My voice disappears on a sob as I realize that I was right all along.

None of this matters.

And we're all gonna die.

Rain

LAMAR AND I STRUGGLE to carry Quint's body out the heavy wooden door and into the darkened hall as the security guards from the entrance make it to the top of the stairs. I fully expect them to shoot us, and I don't even care. I'm not leaving Quint here.

"What the hell happened up here?" the male officer asks.

Lamar has his back to them. He's carrying Quint's legs, and I have him under the armpits. He's so heavy. I lift a knee to help support his weight and feel my jeans soak through with blood as soon as it touches his back. Setting his butt down on the floor, I sit with his upper body in my lap and cry.

"Good Lord, Ms. McCartney. When Mr. Jenkins said he shot an intruder, I didn't realize it was your partner."

"It was my fault," Lamar says, sitting across from me, hugging Quint's shins to his chest. "I shouldn't have gone in there." His face collapses into a broken, silent sob.

"Well …"

The two officers look at each other, perplexed.

"You want us to help you carry him out?" the male officer asks.

I nod. The two cops rush over and each take a shoulder. They lift him off of me, and I miss the weight of him as soon as they do. Taking a leg from Lamar, we share a brief, miserable moment before we carry our brother and best friend down the marble steps, right under the watchful, beady eye of Governor Steele and his collection of sponsors.

When we reach the bottom of the stairs, the female officer hands Quint off to her partner and runs over to the welcome desk to grab my duffel bag.

I don't know why, but their kindness makes it hurt even more.

She opens the door for us and walks us down the front steps and into the twilight.

"Where should we take him?" the male officer grunts, shifting Quint's weight in his arms.

I shake my head. "I don't know."

The sound of anarchy fills the air—motorcycle engines revving, screams, howls, laughter, gunshots.

"How about over there?" his partner suggests, pointing to a dogwood tree in full bloom. "Just until you figure something out."

I nod and shuffle over to the tree in a daze. We lay Quint down beneath it on a bed of pine needles and dogwood petals, and the lady cop places a hand on my shoulder.

"I'm so sorry, Ms. McCartney."

"For what it's worth," her partner adds, his voice gruff and sincere, "that was a damn good interview."

"Thank you." I don't know if I spoke the words or simply thought them, but the officers walk away.

Now, it's just me.

And Lamar.

And a sleeping Quint.

At least, that's what it looks like.

That's what I want to tell myself.

I don't know why, but I reach over and gently peel the Caucasian-colored bandage off his neck.

Then, I snort out something that might almost be a laugh if it wasn't so goddamn painful and ironic.

"His wound is healed."

Lamar sits with his legs crossed and his face buried in his hands. "It was all for nuthin'," he mumbles. "Us livin' in that mall, you takin' care of him, Wes getting' arrested … it was all to save Quint, and now …" He shakes his head as his shoulders begin to rise and fall.

"Maybe this was supposed to happen," I say, rubbing his back like my mom used to rub mine when I was upset. "Maybe it was his destiny."

I don't believe a word I'm saying. And neither does Lamar.

"I don't believe in destiny," he says. "Look around. It's all just fuckin' chaos. It's just bad shit happening to good people. That's all life is. I fuckin' hate it!" he yells on a broken sob.

"Me too."

"I want my mom."

"Me too," I whisper around the swollen lump in my throat.

I wrap my arm around him and pull him close. Quint and Lamar's mama abandoned them when they were little. Rumor has it that their daddy beat her so bad that, one night, she just upped and left. Never heard from her again. But I wouldn't be surprised if that's just a story their daddy made up, and she's really buried out back behind their house somewhere.

Just like my mama.

"I wanna go home."

"Me too, buddy."

But my home isn't in Franklin Springs anymore. It's locked in a cage three blocks away. Wes is my home now, and by this time tomorrow, he'll be gone, too.

Because being good is a terminal disease around here.

Which probably means that I'm next.

I've been a good girl my whole entire life. Straight As and church on Sundays. Smile for the camera. Say *please* and *thank you.* Cheer at your boyfriend's games. Suck his dick when he wants it. Always wear makeup, but not too much makeup. Look pretty, but not too pretty. Tiptoe around your daddy. You know he has issues. Don't drink. Don't smoke. Don't curse. Respect your elders. Do as they say.

That's what my mama taught me. She was as good as they come.

And she was the first one to go.

"Death to sheep," the Bonys say.

How right they are.

As I rub Lamar's back, the neon-orange stripes on my sleeve almost seem to glow in the dark. I follow them up to my shoulder and across my chest.

I might be a sheep, I think. *But this sheep is wearing wolf's clothing.*

"Come on," I say, giving Lamar a squeeze. "Help me pick him up."

"What?" He sniffles, looking up at me with heartbroken brown eyes. "Why? Where are we going?"

"We're going to do something bad."

May 8
Wes

I TAKE A DEEP breath, savoring the scent of burning leaves in the cool fall air until my lungs feel like they're burning too.

The woods are a blazing blur of red and orange as my dirt bike flies over miles and miles of trail. It seems to go on forever, and that's perfectly fucking fine with me. There's no sense of urgency anymore, no doomsday clock, no guillotine hanging over my head. It's just me and my girl and the woods I've called home since I was young enough to have one.

We bounce over a tree root in our path, and Rain giggles in my ear, squeezing me tighter. I used to love the way her tits felt while smashed against me whenever she rode on the back of my bike, but I think I love the way her round belly feels even more.

I suck in another breath and marvel at this fucked up new feeling.

It's not just happiness. I was happy sleeping in a puddle on the floor of an abandoned mall with Rain by my side. No, this is something else.

This is everything else.

All of it. All the things I ever wanted but wasn't stupid enough to hope for. Safety. Security. Love. Life. Fun. Freedom.

A future.

I close my eyes and inhale another lazy lungful of fresh air, but when I open them, I have to slam on the brakes. Rain squeals and clings to me for dear life as I skid sideways and stop inches away from a fifty-foot-long banner as it unfurls from an oak branch and blocks our path.

Like so many banners I've seen before, I expect one of the four horsemen of the apocalypse to be staring down at me—a cloaked demon riding on the back of a smoke-breathing black stallion, ready to chop my head off or light me on fire—but what I find there instead is even more terrifying.

The putrid, pasty scowl of Governor Fuckface. His jowly mouth opens, baring razor-sharp teeth that slam down again and again, missing us by millimeters.

I grab Rain and stumble away from the banner just as my bike disappears into the void of his cavernous mouth. From this distance, I can see the whole image now. It's in similar shades of black and red and gray, like the April 23 banners we all saw in our nightmares, but instead of April 23 at the top, this one simply has a bull's-eye.

Right in the middle of Fuckface's forehead.

His bloodshot eyes dart left and right as his teeth continue to gnash at nothing, but just when I begin to feel like he's no longer a threat, the trees shed their vibrant leaves in a single, sudden explosion. Rust-colored confetti rains from the sky as every tree in the forest begins to age in reverse. They shrink and shrivel up, twisting and contorting until they're nothing but saplings again.

Then, they reach for us.

"Mwa-ha-ha-ha-ha!" The banner man cackles as spindly branches grab for us like claws.

The sky goes dark, and the wind howls through the barren woods as I grab Rain's hand and turn to run back the way we came.

"Wes!" she screams just before her hand is ripped away from mine.

"Rain!" I turn to find her six feet above the ground, suspended in the branches of a sapling.

She's floating in some sort of pink primordial ooze, and the tree appears to be fucking feeding on her, growing bigger and stronger than all the others.

"We must return to the one true law!" Fuckface howls. "The law … of naychuh!"

My vision blurs. My fists ball at my sides. And when he opens his mouth to cackle again, I take off in a sprint. I'm going to rip him down and rip him apart and fucking feed him to himself until he chokes on his own evil hypocrisy, but before I get there, I notice his eyes go wide in fear as they focus on something behind me. I slow to a jog and turn around as people from all walks of life begin to march into the forest. The collective crunch, crunch, crunch *of the leaves under their feet is deafening as they surround us, each one with a fist in the air.*

"Seize them!" Fuckface shouts.

The trees come alive, snatching children from their mother's arms, ripping families apart as they scream and reach for one another. Pink plasma surrounds their tangled, trapped loved ones as the trees feed on their screaming bodies.

*But the people in the woods are undaunted. They continue to march forward, in unison—*crunch, crunch, crunch*—as the bull's-eye in the center of Fuckface's forehead begins to glow like a flashing neon sign.*

I glance at Rain, her face distorted through the ooze, and she begins pointing frantically at something below me.

When I look down, I'm holding her dad's .44 Magnum.

I kiss the barrel and say a silent, Thank you. *Then, I close one eye and aim for the target.*

When I squeeze the trigger, I expect that fucker to disappear, go up in smoke, burn to the ground, something, but instead, he simply laughs at me.

"Mwa-ha-ha-ha-ha!"

I raise my gun and fire three more rounds into that shithead's forehead, but still … nothing.

*Then—*crunch, crunch, crunch*—the sea of men, women, and children behind me step up to join me on the front line. They stand shoulder to shoulder with me, lowering their fists as they draw their* *weapons—shotguns, rifles, flame-throwers, hand grenades—an arsenal as diverse as they are.*

This time, when I raise my gun, they all take aim with me.

This time, when I squeeze my trigger, the entire traumatized, hungry, tired, homeless, grieving, fucked up population fires their weapons alongside me. And this time, when my bullet hits the bull's-eye, it's joined by a thousand others.

The target jerks and flashes and rings like a carnival bell before it explodes in a giant ball of fire. I have to shield myself from the heat as Governor Fuckface lets out a pained, defeated cry.

Gasps and cheers and laughter spread through the crowd, so I lower my arm and watch as the banner burns away. The breeze blows its sparkling ashes around us like swirling silver glitter as the saplings twist and grow and sprout new green leaves.

I run to Rain's tree and catch her in my arms as she leaps from the growing branches. The smile on her face is brighter than fucking sunshine as I spin her around, watching everyone in the woods do the same.

This time, when I inhale, the air doesn't smell like burning leaves.

This time, it smells like burning governor.

I exhale with a content sigh as the sound of knuckles on a steel bar wakes me from my dream.

What the fuck was that? I wonder as I scrub a hand down my face.

I haven't had a dream like that since the government was pumping them into my head, pre–April 23. Of course, those always ended with four demonic horsemen destroying everyone and everything in their path in an apocalyptic blaze of glory, not with the citizens banding together to defeat the enemy. Big fucking improvement.

I open my eyes to find Hoyt standing at my door. He's staring at the floor even harder than usual, his mouth forming a perfect frown. It's not until I see what he's holding that the bliss from my dream wears off and the nightmare that is my fucking reality comes crashing down around me.

It's a bundle of brown.

Fucking.

Burlap.

"The governor moved the Green Mile up to this mornin'." Hoyt clears his throat. " 'Fraid I'm gonna hafta ask you to put these on."

The sadness in his voice makes me have to clear my own fucking throat.

Jesus, Hoyt.

I stand up and approach the bars.

"How long have I got?" I ask, pulling the jumpsuit from Hoyt's reluctant arms.

"Don't know." He sighs and shakes his head, his chin practically resting on his chest.

I notice that he's still holding something—a white plastic cup filled with caramel-colored liquid.

"A little hair of the dog?" I ask, trying to lighten the mood.

Hoyt's eyes jump to mine in a panic. "I … uh … no. I just … thought you might want a fresh cup … you know … to brush your teeth."

He brought me whiskey. Sweet fucking bastard.

"Officer Hoyt, I could kiss you."

I grab the cup from my sink and exchange it for the one in his meaty hands. "Thanks, man."

Hoyt nods at the ground before shuffling away.

I swirl the alcohol around in the cup, taking a deep whiff until his footsteps fade in the distance.

Then, I pour it down the drain and brush my teeth.

I have a date with the fucking devil today.

I'll drink when it's over.

Rain

AFTER LYING WIDE AWAKE next to Lamar's skinny, snoring body all night, I decide I've had enough. If I don't stretch my legs soon, I'm gonna scream, and I don't want to wake Lamar up. I'm sure wherever his mind is right now, it's a hell of a lot better than what's waiting for him here.

Reaching up, I feel around with my hand until it hits a dangling handle. Then, I yank as hard as I can. The lid pops open with a quiet click, and sunlight floods the spacious trunk. We went with a Cadillac this time—at Lamar's request. A metallic purple one sitting on blocks.

I sit up and stretch before climbing out of the trunk, but when I do, a wave of nausea almost brings me back down to the fetal position. The blood on my jeans must have dried and stuck to my skin overnight. Every movement severs the crusty bond a little more—like a bandage being pulled off—and I smell like a corpse.

Once my feet are planted firmly on asphalt again, I suck in a few breaths of fresh air. Then, I turn and unzip the duffel bag as quietly as possible, pulling out a bottle of water Michelle gave me yesterday and a prenatal vitamin.

I just hope I can keep it down.

As I unscrew the cap, Lamar throws an elbow over his face and groans.

"Morning," I mumble, tossing the giant, chalky pill into my mouth. I swallow with a shudder.

"Why's everybody so loud?" he whines, making me realize that it *is* pretty loud out here.

I turn in the direction of soon-to-be Burger Palace Park, and my jaw almost hits the Cadillac's chromed-out bumper. Dozens—no, *hundreds* of people have gathered around our handiwork.

Last night, Lamar and I laid Quint's body in the middle of Plaza Park, his arms and legs spread out like a human X. Then, we went and found the dead Bony I'd seen on the side of the road yesterday. I took his King Burger mask to put over Quint's face, and Lamar took a can of orange spray paint he'd found in the guy's hoodie pocket. Once the bloodstained mask was in place, I painted the words *HERE'S YOUR SPONSOR* in a circle around Quint's body.

"Lamar." I shake his shoulder. "Lamar, look!"

He grumbles and sits up, dreadlocks smashed against the side of his head as he turns and squints in the direction of our human protest sign … and the crowd gathering around it.

"Oh shit …" he says, almost to himself. "It worked."

Turning to me, Lamar's brown eyes go wide. "The sublimi-whatever thing! It worked! People are coming! Holy shit, Rain! What pictures did y'all use?"

"Just some photos I found on Google. People marching with their fists in the air. People rioting in the streets. Oh, and a picture of Governor Steele's banner from the capitol building with a bull's-eye Photoshopped right onto his forehead." I smirk.

Lamar snorts and shakes his head. "You 'member, before all this shit started, you had blonde hair and wore cowboy boots and dresses. Now, look at you." He gestures from my head to my waist. "Black hair. Boned out. Savage as fuck. You're like … Post-Apocalypse Barbie now."

"I feel more like Morning Sickness Barbie," I say with a forced smile. But it fades the moment I let my gaze drift over to the growing crowd circling the body of my dead best friend.

I wrap an arm around Lamar's shoulders and exhale.

"What do we do now that they're here?" he asks.

"I don't know," I say with an honest shrug. "Go start a riot, I guess."

Lamar nods. "For Quint."

"And Wes."

"And your folks." He gives me a sympathetic look.

"And Franklin Springs."

"And all the people pushin' up oak trees down there."

Sliding my free hand into the front pocket of my hoodie, I splay my trembling fingers across the biggest reason of all.

And for you, little one.

My matted hair suddenly blows into my face as a van flies past us on the road, weaving around all the abandoned cars like an Olympic downhill skier. Then, it slams on its brakes with an ear-splitting screech. A second later, the Channel 11 news van backs up next to us. Michelle rolls her tinted window down, revealing a fresh-faced reporter with a sparkle in her eye, an entire tube of concealer covering her bruises, and a breaking story to chase.

"Do you see that crowd?" she shouts. "It worked! Come on! Let's get over there!"

I grab the duffel bag as Lamar climbs out of the trunk. Michelle hops out and opens the giant side door on the van for us.

"Where's Quint?" she asks as we pile inside.

Lamar drops his eyes, and I raise a single finger in the direction of the park.

"Oh, he's already over there?"

"You could say that," I mutter.

Ever the good journalist, Michelle's eyes narrow to slits as they shift back and forth between Lamar and me. It doesn't take her more than a second to deduce from our tear-streaked faces and blood-soaked clothes what happened.

"Oh my God. No."

I nod.

"Quint is …"

I nod.

"Are you serious?"

I nod.

Lamar stares out the window, practically catatonic, as I fill her and Flip in on what happened.

Michelle reaches for the bottle of vodka in her cupholder and takes a long swig as I tell her the story, her red lipstick staying perfectly intact.

"And the governor said they're moving the execution up to this morning?"

After everything I just told her, that's what she's focused on?

"Yeah, but I don't know when."

"Oh my God." Michelle takes another swig. "We have to start broadcasting now. Here, put this on."

She tosses a bundle of soft red material at me. I catch it in my lap as the scent of lavender fabric softener fills the air.

"I grabbed you a wrap dress from my closet since it's kind of one-size-fits-all. It was the best I could do on such short notice." She gives me an apologetic look. "At least it's red—the color of revolution."

"Revolution?"

"You got 'em here. Now, you gotta tell 'em what to do."

All of our heads turn toward the crowd flooding into Plaza Park as we drive past. I can hear their shouts from inside the van as the riot cops with Plexiglas shields try to push people off the field.

My palms begin to sweat as I turn my back to everyone in the van and strip my hoodie off over my head, followed by my once-white tank top. I then pull off my hiking boots and peel my blood-encrusted jeans off my legs. The skin underneath is stained maroon, and fresh tears fill my eyes as images from last night flash before them. Quint's body in my lap. The kindness of the security guards who helped us—I don't even know their names. Holding Lamar as he cried himself to sleep. I consider taking the bottle of water and rinsing my legs clean, but it doesn't matter.

I'll probably be covered in my own blood by the end of the day anyway.

Or Wes's.

With a heavy sigh, I slip on the wrap dress and tie it around my waist. The fabric is soft and clean and somehow comforting.

"Here." Michelle hands me a tube of lipstick and a comb from her purse. "You don't want people to just hear you. You want them to *listen* to you. A bold lip draws their eyes to your mouth."

I remember another woman I saw on TV with a bold red mouth.

"My name is Dr. Marguerite Chapelle. I am the director of the World Health Alliance. If you are seeing this broadcast, congratulations. You are now part of a stronger, healthier, more self-sufficient human race."

I shudder.

We sure as hell listened to her, didn't we?

"What do I even say to them?" I wonder out loud, using the reflective surface of the lipstick cap as a mirror to help me apply it.

Michelle thinks for a minute, vodka sloshing out of her bottle as Flip pulls up onto the curb next to Plaza Park. "I read a study a few years ago about social media that said that people are addicted to outrage. It said that news stories about major events got way fewer likes and shares and comments than posts from people reacting to those events with outrage. We're drawn to that kind of fiery passion. It makes us feel alive, powerful … connected. No successful movement was ever started without outrage, so I say, you get up there and get pissed off."

"I'm not trying to start a movement. I just want these people to help me save Wes."

"What do you think *they* want?" she asks, opening the passenger door to the sounds of chaos and anger. To a sea of people with locked elbows and fists in the air.

I sigh as I yank the comb through my tangled hair. "A revolution."

"You built this bomb, girl. Time to go set it off." Flip winks at me in the rearview mirror before opening his door and climbing out too.

I turn to Lamar. "How do I look?"

He furrows his eyebrows at me, the right one still scarred from the bulldozer accident. "Like a reporter."

"You don't like it?"

"I liked Post-Apocalyptic Barbie better." Lamar shrugs. "Maybe take the hoodie … just in case."

I give him a sad smile as I reach for my sweatshirt. Anything to make him happy. "You doin' okay?" I ask, tying the sleeves around my waist.

He shakes his head and drops his eyes. His chin begins to wobble, but he grits his teeth and squashes it.

"Me too, buddy." I pat his knee. "Me too."

"Guys …" Flip calls out, slapping the side of the van to get our attention. "Looks like we might be too late."

Lamar and I scramble outside and notice that everyone's heads are craned back and tilted to the right as a helicopter descends onto a small, oval-shaped patch of grass next to the capitol building.

Michelle turns to me with an apologetic look on her face. "Shit! I have to get into position. He's gonna go inside the capitol for a minute and then make a big entrance by coming down the capitol steps. I usually meet him at the end of the main walkway and introduce him. Then, we walk over to the park together."

"Introduce him!" I shout, my eyes going wide. "How much time do we have?"

"Before he comes out? Maybe twenty minutes? Thirty, tops."

"Perfect! I'll be right back!" I tighten the sleeves around my waist and take off running.

"Rain! Where are you going?"

"Call me Stella!" I yell over my shoulder.

"*Did I ever tell you you're my heeee-rooooo?*" Elliott sings to me as we jog down the block, take a right, pass the now-maskless dead Bony, take a left, and sprint past the crowd in Plaza Park.

"Ooh! Look at that! My fans await!" Elliott cups his hand and waves at them like the Queen of England as I pull him to a stop next to the news van.

"Michelle," I huff, trying to catch my breath. "Officer Elliott here would like to introduce the governor on today's broadcast."

Michelle narrows her eyes in confusion. Then, she pops them open again once she connects the dots. "Of course! We'd love for you to do the honors, Officer Elliott. Thank you for coming on such short notice. The governor surprised us by moving the execution up, unannounced."

"Tell me about it, honey. We're runnin' around like chickens with our heads cut off over at the station. Got my boy Wes all suited up and ready to go though. He's gon' break some hearts, that one." Elliott shakes his head, and I can tell that one of the hearts is going to be his.

I know the feeling.

"We don't have much time, so I'll cut right to the chase. In a few minutes, the governor is going to walk down those steps, and we need you to—"

"Don't worry 'bout me, honey. I got this!" Officer Elliott interrupts, flicking his fingers at Flip. "Gimme a mic! Where do I stand? How's my hair?" He runs a hand over his perfectly bald head and cackles.

Flip grabs his camera bag out of the van and leads Officer Elliott toward the capitol building as he continues to ramble. Then, glancing behind him at Michelle, he jerks his head in the direction of Plaza Park.

Go. Now, he mouths.

Michelle doesn't hesitate. She leans into the van and grabs a large, padded black bag. Unzipping it, she says, "Lamar … I'm gonna need you to be my cameraman for the day." Turning around, Michelle presents him with a full-size TV camera.

"Oh my God. Can you even hold that thing up?" I ask.

"Pssh." He dismisses me as he accepts the equipment with straining, spindly arms.

"I'll start the broadcast," she says, positioning the camera on his shoulder. "All you have to do is hold it, like this."

"So, is Flip just not gonna turn his camera on or somethin'?" Lamar asks, shifting his weight to support the load.

"That's right. He'll use it to record; it just won't be live. Yours will be."

Turning toward me, Michelle contorts her crimson lips into something I assume is supposed to look reassuring, but her wild eyes are just as manic as the cheering, shouting, fist-pumping crowd swelling behind her. She wants this just as bad as they do. Everyone here has lost someone or something because of Operation April 23, including Michelle. That's why the dream spoke to them, motivated them to pick up their weapons and fight their way down here. The question is, are they here to start a revolution?

Or do they just want their pound of flesh?

"Let's go!" Michelle grins.

She leads the way, squeezing in between Bonys and housewives and pimps and homeless teenagers. "Excuse me!" she yells. "Michelle Ling! Channel 11 Action News!"

But nobody can hear her, and we're starting to get separated.

Somebody grabs my wrist just as she and Lamar disappear through a group of old rednecks carrying hunting rifles. I try to yank my arm away, but the grip is surprisingly strong for a hand so small. I follow the skeletal arm it's attached to up to the face of a woman who's probably in her early forties but looks about fifteen years older. Everything about her is thin—her body, her skin, the limp blonde hair hanging around her sad, wrinkled face.

"Ms. McCartney?" she asks, a pair of familiar green eyes lighting up in recognition. "Oh my God, it *is* you!" She wraps her other hand around my forearm. "You saw my boy yesterday!"

Turning her head, she yells to a rough-looking crew of tattooed men and women behind her, "Y'all! It's the reporter who interviewed my Wesson!"

Her what?

"Ms. McCartney, I'm Wesson Parker's mama, Rhonda. I saw him on the TV yesterday, and I …"

Her face crumples in on itself, and tears spill down her cheeks as my mind struggles to process the words she just said.

Wes's mama.

I never really thought of her as a real person before. More like a ghost. A part of Wes's past that he didn't like to talk about. All I know is that she was a drug addict who neglected her children to the point that Wes's baby sister died of starvation, and she's been in prison ever since.

But here she is, in the flesh. Wes got her eyes, her perfect nose. She must have been so beautiful once.

"You can't let them kill my baby!" Her voice goes shrill as she clings to me for strength. "Please, Ms. McCartney! Please! You gotta help him! That's my boy! My baby boy!"

Tears fill my own eyes as I watch the grandmother of my child beg for the life of her own son. Not only because I share her pain, but also because there's someone else on this planet who loves him. He deserves all the love in the world.

"I'm trying to," I say, not loud enough for anyone to hear over the crowd noise.

"I'm going to!" I shout, shifting my gaze from her to her terrifying group of friends.

They look like they all just got out of prison, which … I realize … they did.

"I'm going to rally everybody to help me, but I need to get to the middle of the crowd first."

Rhonda's eyes—Wes's eyes—fill with hope. "Really?" She jerks my arm. "Really? Did y'all hear that?" she shouts over her shoulder. "Let's get her to the clearing!"

Two big, burly men with facial tattoos and necks wider than my thighs step forward and, without so much as a hello, lift me onto their shoulders.

"Ahh!" I cling to their shaved heads as they push their way through the crowd like human bulldozers, the rest of the released prisoners pushing through behind them.

"Hey!"

"Watch out!"

"Ow!"

"Fuck you!"

Fistfights and shouting matches break out in the wake of my ex-con caravan as the clearing in the center of the crowd gets closer and closer.

The tops of Michelle's and Lamar's heads come into view, and I exhale. They made it. Lamar's camera lens turns to face me, and the red light is already blinking as the bodybuilders barrel their way into the circular opening that has formed around Quint's body.

Michelle is standing on one side of my blood-soaked friend while Lamar stands on the other, trying to keep a brave face.

Poor baby.

Michelle snaps her fingers at Lamar, instructing him to turn the camera toward her.

"This is Michelle Ling, reporting live from Plaza Park minutes before the Green Mile execution event is scheduled to begin. As you can see"—she does a spinning motion with her finger, instructing Lamar to turn the camera in a circle to get footage of the entire crowd—"quite a crowd has gathered here today to express their outrage over what many are calling 'senseless, government-sanctioned murders' and 'public executions for profit.'"

Michelle gestures toward me, and Lamar takes the cue, unsteadily swinging the giant camera in my direction.

"I have our newest reporter, Ms. McCartney, here with the inside scoop on the allegations against Governor Steele and his controversial Green Mile event. Ms. McCartney, can you please tell us why today's execution was rescheduled for this morning?"

I hear her question, but I don't look into the camera, and I don't climb down from my human throne. I don't care about the people sitting at home. They can't help me. The people I need to talk to are right here. Right now.

Sticking the microphone between my teeth, I cling to the stubbled heads of my helpers and slowly push myself to stand on their shoulders. They grab my ankles with their viselike hands, holding me perfectly still as I straighten my spine and look out over the park. Thousands of people have filled the space now, the tops of the saplings barely visible above their heads at the edge of the park. Riot cops line the perimeter, but they're outnumbered a hundred to one. Anger and adrenaline rise off the crowd in waves as thick as steam. It's a deadly powder keg of chaos.

And I'm holding a microphone shaped like a match.

While the crowd quiets to a hush, I scan the sea of faces for one to focus on. I think it will help me feel less nervous if I have one specific person to talk to. But I don't find just one person. I find all the people.

Q and the runaways are front and center, horsing around like little kids. Brad has Not Brad on his shoulders, chicken-fighting Q, whose thighs are wrapped around Tiny Tim's head. Loudmouth and the other runaways I never got a chance to meet are standing in front of them, cheering and trying to help Q win.

A sea of Bonys takes up the left half of the crowd. I pick out The Prez in his fur coat immediately as well as the kids from Pritchard Park who spray-painted our truck—I'd know that helmet with the nails sticking out of it anywhere.

But the person I decide to focus on, the one who makes me think that everything might actually be all right, belongs to an older man with a face like Santa Claus and a body like a grizzly bear. A man I've known my whole life. A man who was more of a father to me than my own sometimes. A man who has a broken leg that I should yell at him for standing on right now.

Mr. Renshaw.

When I lock eyes with him, I don't see anger there. I see forgiveness. Remorse. Understanding. It is not the face of a man whose wife just died. It's the face of a man whose wife did something regrettable, and he's come to make amends for it. Agnes must be okay. And when Jimbo presses his lips together and gives me a single nod, I know we're going to be okay, too.

If we survive what I'm about to do.

Clutching the microphone with two shaky hands, I inhale the crowd's desperation and exhale the terrifying truth. "Today's execution was rescheduled for this morning because Governor Steele has a meeting this afternoon."

The crowd grumbles at the mention of our shared enemy.

"At that meeting, the CEO of Burger Palace is going to pay him five billion dollars to be the official sponsor of the Green Mile execution event."

The grumbles turn to growls.

"They're going to rename this place Burger Palace Park and project King Burger's picture right onto the field. I know this because I heard the governor say it with my own two ears, and so did my friend here … right before he was shot in the back by Governor Steele's bodyguard."

Lamar pans the camera down to his brother's body on the ground and almost drops it as his eyes squeeze shut in pain.

You gotta get through this, buddy. Stay with me.

"How do y'all feel about Governor Steele making five billion dollars for killing our friends and family members—good people—on live TV?"

Fists and shouts fill the air.

"Greed. That's why our species was facing extinction. Not because we were wasting our resources on 'nonproductive citizens,' but because our resources were being hoarded by them!" I shove my finger in the direction of the capitol building, feeling the hands around my lower legs tighten to keep me from falling.

"One percent of our population owns ninety-nine percent of the wealth on this planet! Think about that. That's not nature's way! No other species hoards resources like that. They take what they need, and they leave what they don't. That's the true law that was being violated. This isn't about survival of the fittest; it's about survival of the richest!"

Mr. Renshaw nods his head in agreement, and a surge of pride fills the empty hole in my chest, turning the dark, decaying tissue into something pink and pulsing again.

"Have you seen the governor's mansion?" I ask, shouting as loud as I can.

The people yell and raise their fists in response.

"Your taxes paid for that! Have you seen his fancy new helicopter?" I gesture toward the landing pad behind me.

Their shouts and fists rise up again.

"Well, you bought it for him! Have you seen the CEO of Burger Palace's private island?"

"No!"

"You paid for that, too, when they started charging forty dollars for a King Burger Combo! They're killing us for profit, y'all. And that's what's about to happen right here, right now, to Wesson Parker if we don't rise up and say *enough*!"

The crowd shouts the word, "Enough!" in unison, throwing their fists in the air.

The force of their conviction almost knocks me over. It hits me in the chest like a wrecking ball, overwhelming me with support. I felt like I was fighting this battle on my own for so long, clinging to this person I love tooth and nail while the entire world tried to take him from me. But I'm not alone anymore.

And neither are they.

"The folks who have been murdered here by Governor Steele and his executioner are good people. They're your family, your doctors, your friends, your loved ones. They are people who were willing to die to save someone else."

To save me.

"They are not the enemy. Doing everything we can to help each other survive isn't what made us weak; it's what made us *human*. The real enemy is the one percent of our population who took ninety-nine percent of our resources! The one percent who almost made us go extinct because of their greed. The one percent who killed a quarter of us off through mind control to make up for the lack they'd created and then told us it was our fault for turning our backs on natural selection!"

I lean over and give the microphone to Wes's mom, who's watching me with glistening eyes. *Hold this, please*, I mouth to her.

I untie the sleeves wrapped around my waist and pull the hoodie on over my head, careful not to let my gun fall out of the front pocket. As soon as those orange bones are visible, the left half of the crowd—the side with jackets matching mine—goes wild. I take the microphone back from Rhonda with a hopeful look.

Standing back up, I shove my fist into the air, and when the entire crowd does the same, it feels like the ocean itself is rising up to meet me. Except for Q, who's smirking with her arms folded across her chest.

"They say they want the strongest to survive? Well, I say, there's strength in numbers! Let's show them—"

"Shoot her!" a booming Southern voice shouts from somewhere behind me.

My head swivels in that direction, and I find Governor Steele marching across the capitol lawn, pointing at me in anger, with Officer Elliott and Flip hot on his trail. Three riot cops rush across the street to drag Governor Steele away but not before he produces a gun from somewhere inside his three-piece suit and aims it directly at me.

The brute squad drops me immediately, catching me in their heavily tattooed arms as two bullets whiz through the air over my head.

The microphone slips through my fingers.

And the powder keg explodes.

Rain

THE SECOND THOSE SHOTS are fired, a hundred more follow as the crowd erupts into a pushing, shoving, screaming, stampeding, mindless thing. Michelle, Lamar, and I are swallowed by the mob in an instant. People trample over Quint's body as they push in all directions to get away from the madness. I watch as his mask goes flat under a cowboy boot, and I have to choke down my own vomit.

But there's no time to process. I'm going to end up just like him if I don't stay upright. With every jarring shove, every push and pull, I feel myself getting smaller. It's like that time my parents took me to the beach, and I got sucked away from the shore by the undertow. I remember feeling so weak, my little muscles no match for the all-powerful ocean. The only difference is that if I get pulled under here, I won't drown. I'll have my internal organs liquefied under the stomping, panicking feet of Bonys and rednecks and newly released prisoners.

Shots ring out every few seconds, followed by more screaming, and I don't know if the riot cops are firing at us or if we're firing at the riot cops.

The giant ex-cons who were holding me up are able to force their way through the chaos, but when the crowd closes in behind them, it swallows me whole and forces me under, like a crashing wave.

Fight! I scream at myself. *Stay on your feet!*

Another *ka-pow* reverberates through the air as a man no more than five feet away from me topples into the crowd like a cut tree. I can't get out of the way, and he lands on me, coughing up blood as we both go down.

I scream as I hit the grass under two hundred pounds of bleeding human. "Help! Hellllllp!"

I struggle to roll the dying man off of me as motorcycle boots and cowboy boots and combat boots and hunting boots stomp on my feet and trip over my legs and kick me in the side and crush my arms. Fear and pain hijack my brain as the assault continues. Instead of rolling him off, I pull the dying man back on top of me, using him as a human shield to protect my belly as I try to remember to breathe. Panic grips my throat and squeezes, stealing my voice as it whispers into my ears.

Weak.

Stupid.

Powerless.

Girl.

But then I hear another voice in my ear, one that sounds less like me and more like a female rapper who smokes two packs a day. Faded green dreadlocks tumble into my face as the voice chuckles.

"Bitch, how you gonna start a riot and then lie down and take a nap? That's some gangsta shit right there."

Two hands grab me under the armpits and hoist, lifting me out from under the now-dead body just before another surge of people tramples him as well.

I turn and find the feral, feline eyes of Q staring back at me, a smirk on her full lips and a spatter of blood on her right cheek.

"You came," I mutter in disbelief.

"Pssh. Not from that speech, I didn't." She grins. "Come on. Let's go get ya man."

Before I can ask her how in the hell she thinks we're going to get out of here, Q climbs the bodies around her like a jungle gym.

"Ow!"

"Fuck!"

"What the hell?"

"Come on, you little pussy!" she yells down at me, crawling on top of the angry mob like it's her own personal magic carpet.

I do the same, but much more apologetically, and follow her every move as she crawls on her hands and feet over the undulating sea of bodies. But with the way the crowd is pushing back and forth, we take two steps forward and find ourselves three feet farther away.

"Ugh! Don't these muhfuckas know who you is?"

Q squats on the shoulders of a bearded, plaid-covered redneck and places her fingers in her mouth. The whistle that follows is deafening and brings everyone immediately around us to a halt.

"Y'all need to get dis bitch to the front 'fore I start shootin' muhfuckas just to make a path!"

Everyone's stare shifts from Q to me, and suddenly, a sidewalk of hands, palms up, appears before me.

Q's mouth twists into a self-satisfied sneer as she gestures for me to go ahead.

I give her a grateful nod and begin placing my wobbly knees and shaking hands on their open palms.

"Nah, bitch. Not like dat. Like dis." Q gives me a shove, and I scream and grasp at nothing as I topple over sideways.

But I don't hit the ground. The crowd catches me and carries me like a conveyor belt toward the front of Plaza Park. I blink and try to catch my breath as I wave at Q, who gives me a smug smile before slapping the crap out of the guy she's crouching on for trying to pull her off.

From up here, I can see that droves of angry people are flooding in from the streets—probably thanks to our live broadcast—but the new rioters are only making it harder for the ones trying to flee to get out. Because the longer sides of the park are walled off by risers—which the riot cops are now standing on, firing at anybody who tries to climb up to their level—the only way in and out of the park are the two shorter sides. Folks are either fighting to get out, fighting to get in, or fighting just for the hell of it, but when I see the news van pull away from the curb, I know who's not fighting.

Michelle and Lamar.

I catch a glimpse of Lamar's messy dreadlocks in the passenger side window as the van takes off down the street. I want to feel relieved that they got out, but instead I feel the sudden pull of gravity as a bullet whizzes past me and into the crowd holding me up. I start to fall as everyone around me screams scatters, but I manage to hold onto somebody's shirt to keep my upper body from hitting the ground. When I finally get my feet under me, I notice that the man I was clinging to is standing perfectly still, staring at the ground through a bullet hole in the middle of his hand.

Then, I hear a scream.

It might be mine. I don't even know anymore.

I keep my head down and keep pushing forward. Too low, and I'll get trampled. Too high, and I might get shot. I trip and stumble over other people who have fallen, their bodies reminding me why I have to succeed today.

No more deaths in vain. No more blood spilled on this ground.

Especially not Wes's.

Someone nearby raises her fist in the air and shouts, "Here's your sponsor!" The words I spray-painted around Quint's body.

Emotion squeezes my chest as the people around her do the same.

Chants of, "Here's your sponsor!" spread like a ripple through the crowd, fists pumping and feet stomping.

It gives me an opportunity to get a little lower and weave my way under their raised fists.

Then, a fresh round of panic breaks out. I didn't hear any shots fired, so I'm not sure what the threat is until I see a shiny metal canister spewing smoke careen through the air over my head.

"Tear gaaaasssss!" someone cries, and the pushing starts again.

I'm crushed by bodies moving in all directions as thick smoke pours in, filling what little open space there is left. Just before it gets to me, I pull the neck hole of my hoodie up to my forehead. Then, I yank the hood down past my chin. I can't see anything through the layers of thick black fabric, but I can feel, and I can climb.

Keeping my breaths as shallow as possible, I try to pretend like I'm Q. I climb the jerking, screaming bodies around me until I'm grabbing hair instead of clothing. Then, I move forward. My eyes and nose and throat begin to burn as I blindly crawl over the coughing, crying heads of strangers.

I called them here, I think as stinging tears soak into the black cotton covering my face. *I did this to them.*

Someone in the crowd behind me fires aimlessly into the air, screaming about his eyes, just as something sharp pokes me in the cheek. I reach out and feel leaves. A branch.

A tree!

I yank the hood off my face and peek out of the neck of my sweatshirt just as the person below me succeeds in bucking me off. I tumble to the ground and land on my feet, but the mob pushes me forward, slamming me into the trunk of a recently planted oak tree.

The first of Governor Steele's victims is decaying under this dirt, but I don't have time to think about that.

I have to figure out how the hell to save the next one.

I want to fight my way down the line of saplings until I make it to Wes's hole, but before I can take the first step, another wave of chaos breaks out. I cling to the tree as wailing police sirens get louder and louder and louder, followed by screaming and pushing and shoving worse than anything I've experienced up to this point. Reaching as high as I can, I grab the spindly branches and pull myself into the tree, praying that it will hold my body weight so that I can escape the crowd threatening to rip me to shreds below.

As soon as I climb above them, I see what all the panic is about. A massive tank, as wide as the entire street with a cannon the size of a telephone pole on the front, is charging straight toward the crowd, followed by two police cars and a SWAT SUV. People are climbing all over one another, trying to get out of the way as the tank lurches up over the curb and into the park. I can't see if anyone gets run over, but a chunk of them seems to disappear in front of the tank as it turns and forces itself in between the hole that was dug for Wes's grave and the rest of the mob.

Blue lights spill over everything as the police cars and SWAT utility vehicle pull in behind the tank and form a tight, square barricade around the hole. I notice that the riot cops have moved from their stations on the risers and are now marching up to the cop cars with their shields raised. One by one, they climb on top of the vehicles, facing outward in a ring of human turrets.

No!

My heart thunders in my chest, my hands shake, and my guts twist into violent knots as the driver's side door to one of the police cars opens. Officer Elliott steps out, and with a solemn look on his face, he opens the back door to the cruiser. Governor Steele hoists himself out on the third try, and the car lifts a full six inches higher off the ground before Flip climbs out behind him.

Flip turns on his camera, which I assume is live now that Michelle is nowhere to be seen, and instructs the governor to stand in the center of their barricade with the SWAT vehicle behind him. I expect Officer Elliott to do another introduction, but Governor Steele doesn't give him the chance.

He simply opens his mushy, shapeless mouth and bellows loud enough for me to hear over the madness, "Bailiff, bring out the accused!"

No! No, no, no, no! Somebody, do something! Elliott, please!

But Officer Elliott simply nods his head once, turns, and walks over to the other cruiser. Opening the back door, he reaches in and pulls Wes—*my Wes*—out by the elbow.

His hands are bound behind his back, and he's wearing a burlap jumpsuit.

Not orange. Burlap.

The sight of him dressed like that rips a scream from my body. Somewhere in the crowd, another woman howls in the same heartbroken pitch, and I know his mama sees him, too.

"Elliott, do something!" I shout. "Somebody! Help him!"

But everyone is screaming. The riot cops are shooting people who try to climb onto the vehicles or who shoot at them first. Tear gas canisters are being tossed out like candy. The crowd is surging against the vehicles, making them rock back and forth. No one can possibly hear me.

But still, I scream.

I look to the driver's seat of the patrol car Wes got out of and find Officer Hoyt gripping the steering wheel and staring straight ahead, his eyes at half-mast.

"Hoyt!"

Governor Steele says something I can't hear and motions to the tank. A man steps out of it and walks across the clearing, but it's not until he stands directly in front of Wes and turns to face him that I can tell who it is.

The executioner.

He's wearing an all-black police uniform, and he has on a loose black mask that covers his entire head with two small eyeholes cut out. His hand is on a pistol holstered on his tool belt, and his focus is lasered in on Wes.

My Wes.

"Flip! Flip, do something!"

The cameraman takes his spot off to the side, next to Governor Steele. Everything is moving so fast. The crowd continues to slam against the vehicles in waves, making all but the tank rock back and forth, but with the riot cops standing on top, firing at anyone who climbs too high or shoots at them, nobody is able to do anything to stop them.

My hand dives into the front pocket of my hoodie, and I'm shocked to find my gun still tucked inside.

The moment my finger wraps around the trigger, I'm back outside Huckabee Foods, staring at a beautiful boy in a blue Hawaiian shirt, who is smiling at me with perfect white teeth. His light eyes sparkle under a canopy of black lashes, and I'm lost in them until his face contorts in pain. Blood explodes from his shoulder, and I don't hesitate. I don't think. I grab the machine gun off the dead guard beside me, turn, and pull the trigger, spraying two men and a sliding glass door with enough bullets to take out an entire army of meth-head gangbangers.

I've done this before, I tell myself.

I can do it again.

But I don't have a machine gun this time. And I can't be impulsive.

As the executioner raises his weapon, I realize that I can only get one shot off before the riot cops see me and take me out.

This is it.

I pull the gun out of my pocket.

Time slows down.

And I'm forced to make the hardest decision of my life in an instant.

Assassinate the governor and end the Green Mile once and for all but risk Wes still being executed in the process?

Or kill the executioner and give Wes a chance to escape in the confusion?

His legs aren't shackled. He could slip between the vehicles and disappear into the crowd.

But how many more "accused" would die in his place? How much longer would the governor's reign of terror last?

Do I sacrifice one life to save the others?

Or sacrifice the others to save *the one*?

My one.

My Wes.

My decision is made.

Ten Minutes Earlier
Wes

WHEN HOYT TOLD ME that “Ms. McCartney” came to get Elliott to introduce the governor, I knew she had some shit up her sleeve. When he wordlessly put me in the back of a police cruiser instead of walking me through the tunnel, I knew it must be bad. But when he pulled up behind another cruiser, a SWAT vehicle, and Mac’s fucking tank just to escort me into Plaza Park, that’s when I knew.

That dream was no fucking fluke.

That dream was planted by a certain little black-haired rag doll with a death wish.

As soon as the park comes into view, my mouth falls open in a silent curse. I’ve never seen so many people shoved into one square block before. The entire crowd is fighting and flailing and pounding their fists in the air as tear gas canisters sail overhead, and gunshots loud enough to hear inside Hoyt's bulletproof cruiser ring out.

What the fuck have you done, baby?

I shake my head as adrenaline floods into my extremities, and panic seizes my lungs. My eyes scan the mob, frantically searching for a familiar heart-shaped face, but everything is just a blur of fists and weapons and smoke and mouths twisted in pain and anger.

I told you I'd get out of this. What the fuck have you done?

Hoyt glances at me in the rearview mirror. All the shaggy, unwashed hair in the world couldn't hide the pity and remorse written all over his doughy face. I don't have to pretend to be fucking terrified when I look back at him. I am.

Just not for me.

The tank barrels into the crowd, and the screams of the people in its path bounce off the windshield.

"Goddamn." I cringe and cling to the seat with cuffed hands as people flood into the risers to get out of the way.

Hoyt and the other two vehicles pull into the park behind the tank, and the four of them form a perfect little square.

I don't have to be able to see the ground to know what they're protecting.

My fucking grave.

Hoyt throws the car in park and sits with his thick hands wrapped around the steering wheel. He doesn't move. He doesn't speak. And gauging from the amount of swallowing and throat-clearing he's doing, he's not real happy about what's about to happen.

Or at least, what he *thinks* is about to happen.

Poor bastard. I want to let him in on my plan just to put him out of his misery, but I can't fucking trust him to play along. He's a worse actor than Elliott. Look at him. He can't even pretend to be professional.

My attention is pulled away from Hoyt when I notice riot cops in gas masks, carrying full-body bulletproof shields, marching over to the car. The first three climb directly on top of our cruiser, standing on the hood, the trunk, and the roof.

The fuck?

One by one, cops fill in from the sides of the park until all four vehicles have at least three riot cops standing on top of each.

Governor Fuckface is now standing between the tank and the gaping hole in the ground as Flip lifts a TV camera onto his shoulder and points at him.

As his pasty, bloated face opens and closes, my hands begin to shake.

No! I yell at myself, balling them into fists. *Stop it! You don't fucking end here. You survive, and so does Rain. That's what you do. That's how this shit works.*

But as the crowd surrounds the vehicles and begins rocking them back and forth, including the one I'm presently freaking out in, I realize that I'm not so fucking sure anymore.

Yeah, I have a plan. But I didn't exactly factor in an angry mob or tanks or riot cops or my girl getting trampled to death while I sit here and do nothing either.

I swallow back a surge of bile as Elliott marches over to my door and yanks it open.

Here we go. God, you better fucking have my back.

I step out into a three-hundred-and-sixty-degree assault on my senses. The crowd noise is deafening, the air is thick and humid and tainted with tear gas, and the mid-morning sun is blinding as it bounces off the cruisers and shines directly into my face.

But even through all of the sensations I'm being blasted with, one ear-splitting scream rises over the rest.

She's out there.

She's fucking out there.

Goddamn it.

I don't need this. I need to focus, but now, all I can think about is kicking Elliott right in the fucking face and diving into that crowd, so I can find my girl and drag her ass to safety.

Elliott steers me by the elbow to stand in front of a five-foot-by-five-foot hole in the ground—*oh, look at that; they widened it just for me*—and gives me a little pat on the shoulder before letting me go.

I have to physically shake my head to clear my thoughts of Rain.

Focus, fucker!

I blink and stare straight ahead, finding the cameraman and the devil himself standing across from me with their backs to the SUV.

Governor Fuckface sneers, and I spit at his feet.

"Mistuh Parkuh," he begins, condescension oozing through every missing consonant, "you were arrested on May 5 for allegedly procuring and administering life-saving drugs to a young man with a fatally infected wound. On May 6, you were found guilty of this crime, and as such, you have been sentenced to death."

Someone gets out of the tank behind me. A cop wearing a black executioner's mask trudges past, coming to stand directly across from me. Fuckface is still talking, but I'm searching the man in black for some assurance that this is gonna go down the way I planned.

"I would offuh you a few last words, but as you can see, the little interview you gave yesterday has the *constituency* all riled up. So, I'm afraid those are gonna be the last words you eva get to speak in *my* state, boy. Executionuh"—he steps aside and gestures toward the man in black—"fire at will."

Come on. Come on …

My entire body sways with every forceful pump of blood through my veins as the cop unsnaps his holster and draws his weapon. It's a small handgun, probably a .22—something large enough to kill me without blowing the back of my head off in the process.

How considerate.

I swallow and hold my breath as the executioner lifts the gun and steadies it with the palm of his left hand under the clip. And that's when I notice that every knuckle on both of his hands are as scabbed and mangled as mine.

Mac.

I exhale and close my eyes.

And for a fraction of a second, I'm at peace.

With the blinding sun and flashing blue lights and screaming mob and sinister scowl of pure fucking evil finally blocked out, it's just me and the life I've placed in the bloody hands of a complete stranger.

Until I hear *her.*

Over the roar of the crowd, over the cruisers being rocked back and forth, over the shouted warnings from the riot cops, I hear *her.*

"Somebody, do something!"

She's close. Too fucking close.

My eyelids slam open, and my head swivels automatically in the direction of her voice. Rain is the first thing I see, tangled in the branches of a baby oak tree, just like the dream I had last night. Only she's not being devoured. Quite the opposite. She has her gun raised, and she's aiming it directly at Mac.

Fuck!

Without thinking, I drop to the ground and sweep my leg out, knocking Mac clean off his feet as three gunshots ring out in rapid succession. The first one Mac fired into the air just before he hit the dirt. The second one shattered the passenger window of the SWAT vehicle he was standing in front of, splintering the glass—where his head would have been—like a spiderweb. And the third one came from somewhere to the left of me.

I turn in that direction and find Hoyt standing beside his cruiser, holding a smoking gun over the roof of his car. His face is slack-jawed and wide-eyed, just like the girl in the tree fifty feet behind him. Rain lowers her gun in stunned shock and raises one shaking finger to point at something on the other side of me.

Before I can even turn in that direction, I feel a rush of putrid air ruffle my hair as something hits the ground beside me like a three-hundred-pound sack of rotten potatoes. I swing my head around to find Governor Fuckface lying on the ground, bleeding out from the neck as he coughs and gurgles. His mouth opens and closes like a fish out of water as he holds one of his three chins with one hand and reaches out to me with the other.

"Ew!" Officer Elliott squeals as he walks over and lifts one perfectly polished hard-sole shoe, firmly placing it over the governor's ribs. "Hoyt, did you have to shoot him in the neck? That's so nasty!" With a disgusted grimace and a shove, Elliott rolls Beauregard Steele's gasping body into the hole that was dug for me.

Or was it?

I did notice that it was a little bit wider than usual.

Another man in all-black civilian clothes, like a bodyguard, steps out of the tank and tells the riot cops to stand down. As soon as they holster their weapons, the crowd erupts in cheers. I walk on my knees over to Mac. I can't help him up because my hands are still fucking cuffed behind my back, but he groans and sits up on his own, pulling his mask off in the process.

"You okay, old man?"

He nods and glares at Hoyt, who's now getting a shoulder massage from Elliott.

"You're jealous that he got the kill and not you, aren't you?" I tease.

Mac's jaw grinds, and his eyes narrow as they cut back to me. "Who knew those two clowns would have their own fucking plan?"

I chuckle. "Evidently, my girl had one, too. She damn near blew your head off, man."

"You mean, *that* girl?"

I follow Mac's smirk over my shoulder and find the riot cops helping Rain climb onto the hood of Hoyt's cruiser. She's wearing that fucking red lipstick again, and she has a red skirt or dress or some shit on under her spray-painted, blood-splattered hoodie.

I pull my lip between my teeth and stare as she hops down, the wind ruffling her hair and blowing her skirt up before she lands with a graceful thud just a few feet away from me.

She's here.

She's right fucking here.

I barely register the click of my handcuffs before I'm on my knees with my face buried in my girl's belly and my arms wrapped around her thighs.

"Don't look at me like that, little missy," Mac's deep voice grumbles behind me. "I wasn't gonna kill him."

I laugh. I fucking laugh until I damn near cry as Rain's fingers comb through my hair and her body sinks into my lap and her swollen, red eyes stare through mine.

"Did you get tear-gassed?" I ask, swiping my thumbs over her wet cheeks.

"No, I'm just really happy," she sobs, her red lips splitting into a smile that I've wanted to put on her face since the moment I fucking met her.

I let myself watch her smile for a whole second, maybe two, just long enough for me to take a picture of it with my mind. Then, I kiss that fucking grin right off her face.

Somewhere in the back of my mind, a voice tells me that I need to be careful. Stay vigilant. That my story doesn't end like this. That I don't get to be happy. That my world doesn't work that way.

But I tell that voice to shut the fuck up.

It's a new world now.

And in this world, we can be whatever the fuck we want to be.

Even happy.

EPILOGUE

One Year Later
Rain

I SLIDE THE CAR seat into the red vinyl booth and sit down next to it while Wes goes up to the front to order. Lily smiles back at me as I rock her gently, cooing and kicking her feet under her blanket. She's so incredibly beautiful. Soft brown hair like her daddy—only hers is fuzzier and sticks straight up. She has giant blue eyes, like mine, but hers sparkle with the kind of pure, innocent joy that only someone who didn't live through April 23 can know.

By the time Lily arrived, the world was safe again. Orderly. Militant. After Governor Steele was assassinated, we went from zero laws to martial law in the span of about a week. It turns out that all over the country, members of the military were gearing up for a government takeover. Officer MacArthur and Governor Steele's bodyguard, Jenkins, were in the Green Berets together and had already been in talks with Army officials about organizing a coup in Georgia when Wes suggested that they do it at his execution.

It's kind of hilarious that Officer Hoyt beat them to it.

Georgia was the first state to fall, but after that, the other forty-nine toppled like dominoes. Within a few days, the military completely seized power. Existing laws were reinstated, mandatory curfews were enforced, and the released prisoners were put to work—rebuilding businesses, clearing the roads, cleaning up the graffiti, and burying the dead. It's still weird to see tanks driving down the street every night at 8 p.m. and generals giving press conferences instead of men in ten-thousand-dollar suits, but if it means my daughter and I can go to the grocery store without getting raped, robbed, killed, or kidnapped, I'll take it.

Once the state governments started being overthrown, the president read the writing on the wall and just … disappeared. *Rumor has it that he flew off to Tim Hollis's private island along with a bunch of the other "one-percenters" and is living quite comfortably in the tropics.*

Burger Palace didn't survive though. After Lamar's footage of what happened at Plaza Park made the national news, boycotts and vandalism spread across the country. Here's your sponsor, Fuck your sponsor, Not my sponsor, *or some other variation was spray-painted over every image of King Burger from California to Connecticut.*

After the Burger Palace in Franklin Springs shut down, Mr. and Mrs. Renshaw bought it for cents on the dollar and turned it into a mom-and-pop barbeque joint. They'd actually liked cooking for all the runaways at the mall and decided to try their hand at the service industry. It's the only restaurant in town, so even though it's not the best-tasting barbeque you've ever had—and every once in a while, you might find some buckshot in your brisket—they do a ton of business.

I'm happy for them. I might not ever be on speaking terms with Agnes again, and I still low-key hate her guts, but … I guess we came to some kind of a truce. When Wes kicked them out of my house after the riot, Jimbo forced Agnes to apologize for having Wes arrested and for tying me up, and I apologized for knocking her out and stealing their truck. But I did not *apologize for running over Carter's foot. He deserved that shit.*

Carter ended up getting a job as a police officer, and get this, his first assignment as a rookie is to patrol the area around the Pritchard Park Mall and make sure there's no resurgence of Bony activity. He's a real mall cop now! Q would die! Actually, I'm sure she already knows. Her mattress is probably a regular stop on his route. Gross. They deserve each other.

My phone dings from somewhere inside my diaper bag.

"Hold on, little lady," I say, pinching my munchkin's toes. "I just gotta … err …" I dig around in the bottomless bag as Lily watches me in amusement. "Got it!"

I yank my phone out and illuminate the screen, giggling at Michelle's all-caps text.

> *THREE MONTHS OF MATERNITY LEAVE IS BULLSHIT. IS IT NEXT WEEK YET?*

I smirk and drop the phone back in my bag. I always thought I would go to school to become a nurse like my mama, but I think I've seen enough bloodshed for one lifetime. After the Green Mile riot, Michelle insisted that I keep working as her co-reporter and personal assistant. I couldn't tell her no after everything she'd done for me, but I also realized that I didn't want to. Nobody had ever listened to me until Michelle handed me a tube of red lipstick and a microphone. She showed me that I don't have to roll over and let bad things happen to me anymore. To the people I love. I can fight for them with nothing more than a camera and a press pass.

Only now, I do it under my new name, Rain Parker, instead of Stella McCartney.

My mama's wedding rings gleam on my left hand as I walk my short nails up baby Lily's chubby thigh. I blow a raspberry on her squishy cheek and feel my insides turn to mush when she lets out a tiny, breathy giggle.

I had no idea that Wes had saved Mama's rings for me until he surprised me on Mother's Day, a few days after the assassination. He took me to the Fulton County Courthouse, and in the exact same spot where Governor Steele had sentenced him to death, Officer Marcel Elliott pronounced us husband and wife. When I asked Wes why he wanted to do it there, he said it felt like "a nice fuck you."

And it did. It felt perfect actually. Lamar walked me down the aisle. Officer Hoyt and Officer MacArthur were our maid of honor and best man. Michelle and Flip were in the audience, taking pictures and videos, and Wes even invited his mama, who cried like a baby the whole time.

After Lily was born, Wes had a tattoo artist transform the wilted pink flower on his ribs into a vibrant orange tiger lily. He said he didn't want to be marked by what had happened to his sister anymore. He wanted to move on. And a big part of that was letting his mama back into his life. Rhonda has stepped up and become the mother he and I both needed. She's clean and sober, she has a job and an apartment, and she comes over for dinner every Sunday. We don't let her babysit though. Wes's trust only goes so far. Besides, we have Lamar for that. At least, until he goes off to college.

I turn my head and smile as Wes saunters over. He's wearing his blue Hawaiian shirt—my favorite—and carrying a tray full of the world's most mediocre barbeque. We don't normally eat at the Renshaws' place—things are still pretty tense between us—but today is special. This is the anniversary of the day we met, right here in this very restaurant—or as Wes likes to call it, the day he kidnapped me at gunpoint from Burger Palace. But he knows he saved me that day. I was as lost as a person could possibly be. My house was a crime scene. My parents, the victims. My friends were gone. My boyfriend had abandoned me. I was being jumped by half the town while high as a kite on my daddy's pain pills. And the world was supposed to end in a matter of days. All I wanted to do was stay numb and die.

All Wes wanted was someone to help him survive.

But somehow, together, we figured out how to live.

Wes's full lips curl into a smug grin the second he catches me staring, and my heart does a little backflip. I can't believe I get to keep him. I can't believe we actually got our happily ever af—

Without warning, the lights go out, and the doors on either side of the restaurant burst wide open. Police sirens blare, and blue lights splash across the darkened walls as hundreds of shoving, screaming bodies run full speed into the restaurant. The customers all around us stand up on their chairs and benches, and they're all wearing riot cop gear—gas masks and shields and billy clubs and guns. When I look back at Wes, he's gone, swallowed by the chanting, fist-thrusting mob.

Chairs and punches are thrown at cops. Tear gas and bullets fly into the crowd. Noxious smoke fills the room as Lily begins to cough and cry behind me.

I pull her blanket over her face and stand up on my seat, hugging the car seat to my chest as I try to find Wes in the crowd. I scream his name, but I can't see or hear anything through my own stinging, watering eyes and the painful wails of my baby girl. I get closer to the edge of the crowd, searching through the blinding, burning smoke when someone reaches out and grabs me, pulling me in.

The crush of fighting, clawing, panicking bodies is so forceful that I can't breathe. I can't even move, except when they shove me in one direction or another. Someone climbs onto my back, trying to get above the crowd, and my knees buckle under the weight. I curl my body around Lily's car seat, trying to protect her as feet and fists and billy clubs rain down on my head and back.

"Help!" I scream as loud as I can. "Help! I have a baby!"

Then, two hands reach out from the smoky darkness and grip me by the shoulders.

"Baby," Wes whispers, gently shaking me. "You fell asleep nursing again."

I open my eyes with a gasp to find a shirtless green-eyed man smiling down at me and a sleeping infant in my arms.

"Oh my God," I cry, clutching Lily to my chest. "Oh, thank God." My heart is pounding as my brain sluggishly tries to grasp the fact that we're not going to be trampled to death.

"Another nightmare?" Wes asks, his dark eyebrows pulling together as he crouches down next to me.

I'm sitting in a rocking chair in my old bedroom—Lily's room now—in the dark. My white nursing gown seems to glow in the moonlight, and my breast is still exposed from her midnight feeding.

I nod and reach a hand out to cup Wes's concerned face. I thought the nightmares would go away after April 23, but they're just different now. Instead of demonic horsemen, it's real monsters. Ones we've already defeated whose ghosts now haunt us while we sleep.

But that's okay. As long as I get to wake up in this beautiful dream, I don't mind a few nightmares now and then.

"You okay?"

I smile and nod again. "Better than I was a few minutes ago," I whisper, echoing the flirty response he gave me from inside his jail cell.

Wes smiles and kisses me on the forehead. "Here, I'll put her down."

He scoops the sleeping bundle out of my arms, and I watch, awestruck, as he lazily carries her across the room. She's barely the size of one of his biceps, but he's so gentle and loving with her. He kisses her fuzzy head before laying her down in the middle of her crib, his back muscles rippling as he leans over. Wes is wearing nothing but a pair of gray sweatpants, and when he turns to face me, his lips curl into a sinister smirk. I follow his gaze down to my chest and laugh silently as I go to pull my nursing gown back up.

"Don't you dare," Wes growls, stalking toward me.

He started a construction company, rebuilding houses that had been damaged during Operation April 23, and one of the perks of the job is this body. Good Lord. He was cut before, but now he belongs on the cover of a romance novel.

A really gritty one where the hero has tattoos and drives a motorcycle and cusses a lot.

Wes reaches his hands out, and I take them, letting him pull me to my feet. Then, I let out a surprised yelp as he grabs my fuller than usual ass and lifts me off the ground. My legs wrap around his waist, and my arms wrap around his shoulders as he chuckles softly, smiling against my parted lips.

"How long until she wakes up?" he whispers, carrying me out of the nursery.

I cringe as we walk past Lamar's room, thankful that his door is shut and lights are off.

"Two or three hours, depending on how long I was asleep."

"Challenge accepted." He smirks, kicking the master bedroom door shut behind him.

When we moved back in, we got all new furniture, painted the walls a dark gray, and I even had a pastor from my old church come and say a blessing, just in case. We made it our own, and I love it. It's not *home*—Wes is my home—but it's not scary anymore either. It's just a house—wood and nails and screws and paint … and bedroom doors that lock.

Holding me up with one arm, Wes turns the silvery latch on the doorknob. The *click* sends an excited shiver down my spine. I tighten my thighs around his waist and let my longer hair fall around us as I tilt my head down to kiss his parted lips. Wes captures my mouth with an appreciative moan. Squeezing my ass with one hand, he reaches up and hooks a finger into the top edge of my nursing gown, yanking the stretchy, gauzy white fabric down until my other breast is exposed as well.

"That's better," he murmurs into my mouth as his rough palm caresses my tender, swollen flesh.

I arch my back as his thumb swirls around my oversensitized nipple, breaking our kiss and allowing Wes to suck and nip his way along my jaw and neck.

I can feel him pressed against me through his sweatpants, so reaching between us, I slide my fingers into his waistband and shimmy it down over his swollen length. Hot, velvety flesh fills my hand, and I lick my lips as I pump him slowly.

"Fuck," Wes growls, his teeth scraping my collarbone as he grabs my ass with both hands again. "I want you just like this."

I squeal as he pushes away from the door, tightening my grip around his broad shoulders as he crosses the room and sits on the edge of the bed. I land on his lap with my knees spread on either side of him and moan when he bends me backward and pulls one straining pink nipple into his mouth. His heavy cock presses against my slippery center, and my hips grind against it instinctively, needing more.

Wes's tongue swirls and flicks and sucks until my breasts begin to tingle and burn.

"Wes!" I hiss, trying to pull away, but he only chuckles and continues his assault. Milk drips from my other nipple and down my breast as I grab his head and try to pull him off me. "Wes, you're gonna get milk in your—"

Holding my stare with blazing emerald eyes, Wes slowly drags the flat of his tongue over my nipple, collecting every drop of milk that falls.

Swallowing, he brings his lips back to my mouth. "I told you …" he rasps, lifting my ass until the head of his cock drags through my folds and presses against my entrance. "I want you just … like … this."

I sink down onto him as he claims my mouth, swirling and exploring with his expert tongue as he guides my body up and down his length. I run my fingers through his hair and cup his chiseled face in my hands as I kiss the mouth that he worships me with.

I don't deserve him. I don't deserve a love like this. It overwhelms me, filling me up until I spill over, milk dripping from my breasts and tears cascading down my cheeks as I come again and again into the night.

But my husband doesn't care. He licks up every drop that I spill and fills me up again.

That's the thing about life after April 23. When you fall in love at the end of the world, you live every day like it's your last.

At least, until the baby wakes up.

I hope you enjoyed The Rain Trilogy! If you did, I think you'll love SKIN. *It's a gritty, taboo, forbidden love story full of '90s nostalgia, dark humor, and heart-wrenching teenage angst. Plus, the entire 44 Chapters About 4 Men series is being adapted into a steamy dramedy for Netflix called* Sex/Life*! Read on for a sneak peek!*
mybook.to/bbeastonskin

SKIN
Chapter One

POSITIVE, POSITIVE, POSITIVE.

It was my first day of tenth grade, and I was *not* going to be nervous. I was going to think deliriously happy, positive thoughts. I was going to skip down the familiar halls of Peach State High School with a bounce in my steel-toed step and a self-confident smirk on my face because *this* was going to be the year that Lance Hightower finally proclaimed his undying love for me. It just *had* to be.

I wasn't going to beat myself up about the fact that I had been trying and failing to make out with that boy since middle school, *nor* was I going to focus on the fact that I still had zero breasts at the age of fifteen. No, I was going to fantasize about all the wildly spontaneous, highly public ways Lance might choose to propose. After all, I'd just learned—thanks to my dad's unhealthy obsession with watching CNN—that it was totally legal for teenagers to get married in Georgia as long as they had written permission from one of their parents. That wouldn't be a problem for me, seeing as how I'd perfected my mom's signature by the age of twelve.

I was also feeling pretty damn good because I knew I'd picked out the *perfect* back-to-school outfit. My trademark black combat boots and wingtip eyeliner were firmly in place; I was rocking some kick-ass black spiderweb fishnets under my favorite pair of too-short-for-school cutoff jeans; my gray midriff T-shirt boasted the logo of an indie band I was absolutely *certain* no one had heard of; and my arms were practically pinned to my sides with the weight of a thousand metal, beaded, and leather bracelets. Also, I'd started smoking over the summer (for real this time), and my shorter, edgier, more angled haircut got tons of compliments, even from Lance (which was the whole point).

Of course, all my positivity went to shit as soon as I made it to the church parking lot for a smoke between classes.

It was no secret at Peach State High School that if you wanted to do something bad, all you had to do was walk out past the rust buckets in the student parking lot, step over a guardrail, and clear the tree line. That was it. On the other side, you would find yourself in a magical wooded wonderland called *the church parking lot*, a place where kids could escape the oppression of our overcrowded, underfunded public learning institution to laugh, smoke, and be merry (if only for seven minutes at a time). The church was a long, abandoned one-room chapel that was in the process of being reclaimed by the forest, and its parking lot was nothing more than a patch of gravel, but to a band of misfit teenagers, it was heaven.

Or so I'd heard. I'd never actually ventured out to the church parking lot during school hours before, but this was my year. I just knew that on the other side of those woods, I'd find *my people*. Artsy, quirky, free spirits who shared my appreciation for alternative rock, avant-garde art, and experimental photography. The group that would embrace me with open arms, invite me to sit with them at lunch, and host raging keggers like the ones I saw on TV.

Instead, what I found was the most intimidating group of human beings I'd ever seen in one place. *Fuck me.* Those kids were cool with a capital *C* and twenty-seven *O*s. They had *multicolored* hair. They had *piercings*. They had expertly painted red lips that I could never pull off with my redheaded complexion. And the accessories—more chokers and studded belts than you could shake a flannel shirt at. One girl was even wearing denim overalls with the legs cut off and one shoulder strap undone. I wasn't punk rock; I was Punky fucking Brewster.

At least my combat boots were vintage and my eyeliner was flawless. That I knew for sure. I'd been perfecting that goddamn cat eye since the age of ten. As long as I kept my grades up, my hippie parents never really gave a shit how much makeup I wore, or what I dressed like, or how many F-bombs I dropped at the dinner table. (And by dinner table, I mean, my TV tray in the living room.) So I stood on the periphery and tried not to stare, clinging to both my Camel Light and the hope that someone would at least admire my eyeliner art.

I watched the guys all squeezing and kneading and nuzzling their girlfriends, and I watched their girlfriends' giant boobs bounce with every giggle.

I bet they have sex, I thought. *Every one of them.*

My face and neck suddenly felt itchy and hot.

Annnnd, now I'm blushing. Fantastic.

I dropped my head and stared down at my boots, which I could see with no problem at all, thanks to my complete and total lack of breasts.

Why can't the heroin-chic look still be in? Maybe it'll make a comeback. Please let it make a comeback.

Everyone out there looked like Drew Barrymore, and I looked like somebody drew a smiley face and freckles on one of Drew Barrymore's pinkie fingers.

My BFF, Juliet Iha, was supposed to be meeting me out there, but after a few minutes, it became pretty clear that she'd flaked out on me yet again.

She's probably out here somewhere, fogging up Tony's car windows.

Juliet was dating a grown-ass man who'd dropped out of high school at least a decade prior and never seemed to have anywhere pressing to be. Without fail, that creepy fucker always seemed to be lurking around wherever we were, leaning up against his busted-ass, old Corvette like an actor cast to play the part of Potential Child Molester in a PSA from 1985. Tony definitely gave me the "no feeling," but Juliet really liked him, and he was old enough to buy us cigarettes, so I kept my mouth shut.

Just as I was about to stamp out my Camel Light and drag my sad ass back inside, I felt two solid arms wrap around my body from behind. One snaked around my rib cage, and the other hoisted me up from behind my knees. Before I could scream, *Rape!* I was flipped completely upside down and plopped, ass up, on the shoulder of a giant. It wasn't until he swatted my backside and laughed in that glorious, soft tone that made my body go all warm and bubbly that I realized I'd been captured by my immortal beloved, Lance Hightower.

Lance Motherfucking Hightower. God, he was perfection. Lance was in my grade, but he was easily half a foot taller than most of the upperclassmen and already filled out like a man. Dude had a permanent five o'clock shadow at the age of fifteen. Despite having the dark, chiseled features of a Disney prince, Lance was a punk rock icon. Every day, he sported the same effortlessly badass look: faded black Converse, faded black jeans, and a faded black hoodie covered in patches advertising obscure European underground punk bands and anarchist political statements that he painted on with Wite-Out during class. That hoodie was so well known, it probably had its own fanzine.

Topping off all that faded black packaging was an equally faded, slightly grown-out green Mohawk. It probably would have added another three inches to Lance's already six-foot-three-inch frame if he ever bothered to style it, and the color totally brought out the green flecks in his coppery-hazel eyes.

Oh, Lance. I had been obsessing over him since the sixth grade. I admired him from afar until last year when we fatefully wound up sharing a pottery wheel in art class. The flirting that ensued was incendiary. Atomic. The only problem was that I was technically "dating" his best friend, Colton, at the time, so things never really got off the ground.

Then, a goddamn miracle happened. Colton upped and moved to Las Vegas to live with his dad right in the middle of the spring semester. I pretended to be sad for a few hours, out of respect. Then, I immediately resumed my campaign to become the mother of Lance's children. The only problem was that Lance and I didn't have any classes together, so all of my flirting had to be done in seven-minute increments between periods. But in tenth grade, what I was sure would be the best year ever, Lance and I had been assigned to the same motherfucking lunch period. I was going to be sporting his last name by May. I just knew it.

"Lance! What are you doing?" I giggled. "Put me down! I can't breathe with your shoulder in my stomach!"

Lance chuckled. "That's so sweet. You take my breath away too, girl."

God, his voice. Like fucking angel bells. For such a big dude with such an in-your-face look, Lance's voice was surprisingly soft and flirty. It was a total mindfuck the first few times I'd heard that sweet sound come out of that ruggedly handsome face. And the pick-up lines. I swear to Jesus he had a new one every time I saw him. I fucking loved Lance Hightower.

I giggled harder, which made my stomach hurt even worse, and swatted at his perfect, patch-covered ass. "Put me down, asshole!"

Before he could comply, we heard a sickening smack from across the parking lot, followed by a deep voice shouting, "Say it again, motherfucker!"

Lance held on tight to the backs of my thighs and swung around to face the commotion, making me even dizzier as I grabbed his waist and peeked around his side to see what was going on.

Although I couldn't make out exactly what was happening due to the blood rushing into my eyeballs, I recognized the assailant immediately. I'd never met him, but I'd heard stories. Everybody had. He was "the skinhead," the only one at our entire four-thousand-student suburban high school.

I'd noticed him in ninth grade because he was literally the only person I'd ever seen wear suspenders (skinny ones, called braces) to school. In a world full of studded belts and chain wallets, that motherfucker wore suspenders—the epitome of dorkiness—and made them look as scary as the stripes on a venomous snake.

A snake who was standing about thirty feet away, looming over a little skater boy who was clutching his rapidly swelling jaw and trying not to cry.

When the kid didn't say whatever it was the skinhead wanted to hear, he buried his fist deep in Skater Boy's stomach, causing him to lurch forward and release a noise so guttural, I assumed something important must have ruptured.

With his left hand, the skinhead yanked the guy's head back by his chin-length brown hair and screamed into his terrified face, "Say that shit again!"

I felt like I might throw up. My heart was racing, and my head was pounding from being upside down, but all I could register was a sickening sense of helplessness and humiliation for that poor kid. I'd been raised in a house with pacifist parents and no siblings. I'd never seen anyone get hit before—at least, not in real life—and I felt that punch as if it had been dealt directly to me.

In a way, it had. That punch shook me to my core. It showed me that senseless violence and cruelty really did exist, and they came wearing boots and braces.

When Skater Boy remained silent, the skinhead responded by shoving his head so hard that he flew sideways and landed, hands- and face-first, in the gravel. His body slid a few feet before finally coming to a stop. The kid scrambled to pull himself into a ball and made little screeching sounds as if struggling to suppress a scream.

Instead of attacking again, his assailant began to circle him slowly, like a hawk. I held my breath and gripped Lance's waist tighter, ignoring the throbbing in my eyeballs, and watched upside down as he assessed his victim. I was horrified by how calm he was. He wasn't angry or upset, just … calculating. Cold and calculating.

The skinhead approached the kid, who was now trembling and sobbing quietly, and slowly rolled him onto his side with one very heavy-looking combat boot. Still curled up tightly, Skater Boy choked out what sounded like a muffled, garbled apology. Unimpressed, his attacker bent down toward the kid's face and placed a meaty hand firmly on the side of his head. I didn't know what he was doing at first, but when the brown-haired kid started screaming in pain, I realized that the skinhead was pressing his face into the gravel.

"What was that?" he asked calmly, tilting his head to one side as if genuinely interested, the veins in his muscular arm beginning to bulge as he applied more pressure.

"I'm sorry! I'm sorry! I didn't mean it! Please stop! Please!" The scream at the end of his apology got increasingly louder as that heartless, hairless demon crushed his face further into the jagged rocks.

The skinhead released Skater Boy's head and stood up. I exhaled and felt my body relax into Lance's shoulder and then watched in disbelief as he kicked the kid directly in the lower back one, two, three times. By the time my eyes registered the strikes and my ears registered the resulting scream, it was over, but my spirit was forever changed.

It said, *These people fuck and they fight and you'd better get used to it, little girl.*

Lance set me down, slowly, and I wrapped myself around him like a tree trunk for stability.

I stared, partially hidden behind Lance's sturdy frame, as the skinhead idly spit on the ground next to his victim, lit a cigarette, and walked with long, confident strides … directly toward me. The gravel crunched under the weight of his steel-toed boots, which emerged from the bottom of a tightly rolled pair of blue jeans. Bright red laces wound themselves up the front of his boots, and bright red braces slashed across his muscular chest—a chest which was wrapped in a tight black T-shirt emblazoned with the word *Lonsdale.*

Steeling myself behind Lance's comforting presence, I mustered the courage to peek up at the skinhead's face. It was like looking at a ghost. He resembled a person, but there was no color to help differentiate his features. His skin was white. His hair and eyelashes were virtually transparent, and his eyes … his eyes were a ghostly, icy gray-blue. Like a zombie's. And when they landed on mine, my hair stood up on end so violently, it felt like a million tiny needles were stabbing me at once.

Those zombie eyes flicked from mine to Lance's with a look of irritation as he approached. I could feel a buzzing electric current of malice radiating off of him well before he reached us, and I winced as he passed, as if bracing myself for his wrath. When nothing happened, I carefully opened my eyes, relieved by the change in the atmosphere. The static charge was gone. *He* was gone. But he left a broken boy, a still-burning Marlboro Red, and my scattered wits on the ground in his wake.

As traumatizing as my first smoke break had been, that wasn't the reason I was having trouble concentrating in my honors economics class. It was because as soon as the bell rang, I knew I was going to have lunch with Lance Motherfucking Hightower—and my best friends, Juliet and August—but mostly *Lance Motherfucking Hightower.*

I saw the teacher's mouth moving, but all I could hear were my own racing thoughts. *I'm totally going to sit next to him. But what if I get there first? Will he sit next to me? Maybe I should hide and wait for Lance to sit down and then run over and sit next to him before anyone else has a chance. Yes. Totally. Then, I'll find an excuse to touch him. And I'll laugh at all his jokes. Not that it'll be hard. He's so funny. And beautiful. And tall. And edgy. And fucking dreamy.*

When the bell finally rang, I jumped up as if my ass were on fire and sprinted to the bathroom to touch up my makeup.

Then, I hightailed it to the cafeteria to scope out the cool-kid table. Every punk, goth, druggie, drama nerd, vegan, hippie, skater, and metal head at our high school wanted a spot at that table, and even though he was only in tenth grade, Lance was the reigning king of them all. Getting a spot next to him was going to be tricky.

When I ran up, I realized that not only had Lance already taken his seat—right in the middle of the fifteen-foot-long table—but goddamn Colton Hart was also sitting right next to him.

Shit.

Shit, fuck, damn.

When the hell did he get back?

Colton was going to be a major fucking obstacle in my quest to become Mrs. Hightower. He was the world's biggest cockblocker—that was actually how I'd wound up dating him in the first place. He'd just kept inserting himself between Lance and me until I gave in and let him kiss me. Which he did. A lot. Don't get me wrong; making out with Colton Hart was a spectacular way to spend an afternoon. He was super fucking cute. And cocky. And sarcastic. And *bad.* But he just wasn't Lance.

But technically, he *was* still my boyfriend.

Oh my God. What if he thinks we're still a couple? No. There's no way. He never even called me after he left. He probably screwed all kinds of future strippers while he was living with his dad and brother in Las Vegas, and now, I'm small potatoes. I'm just the girl he left back in Georgia who wouldn't let him touch her boobs. It's totally fine. No. Big. Deal.

As I walked up, I couldn't help but admit to myself that he did look damn good. Better than I'd remembered. He was like a wicked Peter Pan. Spiky brown hair with blond tips, pointy ears, perfect male model smile. When he'd left, he'd had a definite punk rock style, like a mini Lance, but I guessed his skateboarding older brother had worn off on him while he was in Vegas. Colton had traded in his boots for a pair of shell-toed

Adidas, his bondage pants for a pair of black cargo shorts, and his studded belt for a chain wallet.

There was a spot open next to both of them, but I made sure to sit next to Lance just to establish whose girl I was. Or at least, whose girl I wanted to be.

As soon as I walked up and set down my backpack, Colton cried, "Kitten! Get your ass over here!"

I glanced down at Lance, who made no attempt to rescue me, and sighed. Getting up and walking around him, I embraced Colton, who had stood up and was waiting for me with open arms.

Feigning excitement, I said, "Hey, Colton! Oh my God! When did you get back?" as he squeezed the shit out of me.

"Last week," he said, rocking me from side to side. "My moms got lonely. What can I say? Living without me is hard." He pulled away and gave me a wink. "Isn't it?"

I rolled my eyes in response, but I couldn't help my traitorous smile. He really was cute. And he smelled squeaky clean. Like a girl. Colton had a thing for products—hair products, skin products. He was vain as hell and proud of it.

After giving me the once-over, Colton whistled. "Look at you. You're making me wonder why I left in the first place." I blushed and looked at the ground. "You wanna ride the bus home with me this afternoon? Just like old times? My mom just stocked the fridge with PBR …"

Yes. No. Kinda?

Before I could say something stupid, Juliet swooped in and rescued me. "She's riding home with me, Colton. BB is *my* bitch now."

Juliet set her tray down across from my backpack and glared at Colton. She never liked him. For starters, I'd kind of forgotten she existed after he and I started dating. I just started riding the bus home with him every day instead of her—a dick move, I knew, but I was fourteen, and he was my first real boyfriend. I was pretty sure "first real boyfriend" would be accepted as just cause for a temporary insanity plea in a court of law. But Juliet also hated him because I'd kind of blabbed to her about how hard he'd been pressuring me to do *stuff* with him. I would have given in, too, if he hadn't told me he was moving. I was *not* giving it up to somebody who was just going to leave in a few weeks. Besides, I was saving myself for Lance Hightower.

Colton glared back at her for a minute. Then, he smiled and asked, "Can I watch?"

We all laughed, even Lance, who was watching the show with piqued interest. When I sat back down next to him (and away from the pheromone cloud that was Colton Hart), I let out a shaky breath and stared straight ahead at Juliet, thanking her silently. Lance, who had resumed his conversation with Colton, reached under the table and gave my thigh a reassuring squeeze. He left his hand there, and I prayed to every deity I'd ever learned the names of that he would slide it up a little farther. He didn't, but he did absentmindedly lace his fingers through the holes in my fishnets as he spoke, causing me to stop breathing long enough to almost actually fucking die.

My mind was sufficiently scrambled when August, whom I hadn't even noticed, spoke to me from the spot next to Juliet.

I had been friends with August Embry since first grade, when we wound up in the same first grade class. Back then, he was a shy, pudgy little thing with no friends, and I was a bossy, talkative little thing with no friends, so we'd just clicked. I loved him like a brother.

August was still a shy, round little thing. He hid his warm chocolate-brown eyes behind a curtain of dyed black hair, and every night, he painted his fingernails black to match. Of course, every day, he would pick them clean again—leaving little black flecks behind, like a trail of breadcrumbs everywhere he went. August was the sweetest, most sensitive person I'd ever met.

I could tell from his body language that August wasn't exactly happy to see Colton either. He and Lance had become kind of close since Colton left. They both liked the same terrible music and competed over who had the best, rarest punk records in their collections, so Lance getting his best friend back didn't bode well for August.

"Hey, A!" I cheered, trying way too hard to sound like a girl who *didn't* have a boy's fingers stroking her inner thigh at that exact moment. "I didn't know you had this lunch period too! Are you growing your hair out? I love it!"

August just smiled and looked down at the food on his tray, which he suddenly decided needed rearranging.

I turned to ask Juliet if I could ride home with her and Tony, but she was gone. Her stuff was still on the table though, and I thought I could hear the sound of her voice. As much as it killed me, I moved Lance's hand so that I could peek under the table. There she was, sitting cross-legged on the floor, talking on her cell phone, which was strictly forbidden at school. There was only one person she could possibly be talking to.

"Juliet," I whispered.

She looked up, annoyed. "What?"

"Ask Tony if he minds giving me a ride this afternoon."

She winked at me and whispered into her brick-sized Nokia, "Hey. BB's gonna ride home with us this afternoon, okay?" She gave me a thumbs-up after hearing his response.

Cool.

Just then, I felt Lance's hand press down on the back of my head and saw his crotch rise up to meet the side of my face. I screamed and tried to sit up, causing my head to smash Lance's hand into the underside of the table. Laughter erupted from the cafeteria as I emerged, red-faced, looking like a girl who'd just eaten a punk rocker's cock for lunch.

I glared at Lance, trying my best to look angry, but his eyes were shut, and he was laughing so hard, he wasn't even making noise. Just the sight of that giant, Mohawked motherfucker smiling ear to ear had me reduced to a puddle of swoon juice in an instant. I burst out laughing right along with him and anxiously glanced over at Colton.

He was laughing, too, but his smile didn't quite reach his eyes. Guess he didn't appreciate the entire lunchroom thinking *his* girlfriend was giving his best friend a BJ under the table.

In that moment, I knew that Colton wasn't going to be a problem. Lance had just established, with dramatic flair and in front of everyone, that I was his girl.

All the hope and hormones had my insides on the verge of spontaneous combustion, so I barely noticed the loud *slam* that came from somewhere behind me. I hardly felt the resulting shudder that rippled down the length of the lunch table. And I didn't turn to look for the source until the faces of all my friends fell and glanced anxiously over my shoulder. Swiveling around on my stool, I followed everyone's gaze to an empty seat at the end of the table.

Um, anyway. Where was I? Oh, right. Planning my spring wedding …

That afternoon, I fought against the current of teenagers fleeing the building, dragging my swollen backpack behind me by one strap, in search of my new locker. According to my homeroom teacher, my old one had to be torn out over the summer to make room for the new science lab. She had given me a little slip of paper with my new locker number and combination on it, saying only that it was "somewhere over on C Hall." I couldn't wait to find that shit so that I could finally offload a few of the ten-pound textbooks I'd been given that day.

Clutching the piece of paper with my new digits on it, I scanned dozens of identical metal doors until I found the one I'd been assigned. It was almost at the end of the hallway, of course, near the exit doors that led out to the student parking lot. I felt relief wash over me immediately.

My first day of tenth grade was a wrap, and overall, it had been a smashing success. I'd smoked with the coolest of the cool kids; wound up with the same lunch period as Lance, Juliet, and August; got a bunch of compliments on my fishnets and new haircut; and now, I had a new locker on the same hall as all the seniors. Okay, so maybe it took me a few attempts to get my code to work, but once that shit was open, it was glorious.

As I bent over to take the last load of books out of my straining backpack, I stopped short, paralyzed by the sight of two black steel-toed boots with blood-red laces planted just inches away from my face … and pointing directly at me.

Fuck.

Fuck, fuck, fuck.

Not him. Anyone but him.

I took my time gathering my stuff, hoping that ignoring him would make him magically disappear. When I finally stood up, arms full of books, I mustered all the courage I had and looked him in the eye.

Zombie eyes. God, his irises were such a pale, pale gray-blue that his pupils looked like two endless black holes in contrast. Two black holes that were sucking me in.

Speak dumbass!

"Um, hey," I said in a voice that didn't sound like it belonged to me.

He didn't reply. He simply cocked his head to the side and studied me with those cold, dead eyes. It was the same way he'd looked at the kid in the parking lot, right before he smashed his face into the ground.

Swallowing hard, I forced myself to break the silence.

"I'm sorry, do you need something?" I squeaked out, trying to sound cute and tiny. I blinked and opened my eyes a little wider, feeling like a woodland creature in danger of being squished by a massive black boot.

"Your shit is in front of my locker," he said. His voice was deep and clear and humorless.

"Oh my God! I'm so sorry!" Tripping over myself, I slid my lightened backpack behind me with my foot.

The skinhead immediately grasped the metal latch on the locker beside mine and gave the lower left corner of the door a swift kick, causing the fucker to pop right open, no code necessary. I shuddered involuntarily as my mind conjured images of that same boot landing square in the back of a scared little skater boy just a few hours earlier.

Afraid that he could smell my fear, I quickly hid my face behind the metal door of my own locker, busying myself by arranging my books and notebooks by size, color, the Dewey fucking decimal system, *anything.* Then, something occurred to me. Before I knew it, my stupid mouth was moving.

"Shouldn't you be suspended?"

I felt my face blush crimson as the blond with the buzzcut slammed his locker shut and asked, point blank, "Why?"

Was he teasing me? We both knew what the fuck he had done.

"That, that fight. Today. In the church parking lot," I said into my locker.

Thinking about that … *attack* had my blood pumping into my extremities and my mind screaming for me to run. I turned and went back to my organizing, hoping to conceal the terror and embarrassment that I was sure my big, dumb doe eyes were doing a shit job of concealing. My face always snitched on me, broadcasting my every thought. My every feeling.

My thin metal makeshift shield vibrated as he spoke, "I didn't get suspended for the same reason you're not sitting in detention right now for smoking. That shit happened off-campus."

"Is he okay?"

God! My fucking mouth! Filter, BB. Filter!

"Who? That little pussy wipe from the parking lot? He'll be pissing blood for a week, but he'll live."

Slowly, the door I had been cowering behind began to close. Moving out of the way so that the metal wouldn't graze my face, I reluctantly turned toward the boy with the cadaverous eyes, who was deliberately pushing my locker shut. Once the door was firmly closed and I had nowhere left to hide, Zombie Eyes leaned toward me and reached around my body with his left hand. I squeezed my eyelids shut and braced myself for something violent and potentially bloody to happen.

With his voice lowered so that only I could hear, he said, "If you hit a fucker in the kidney hard enough … right here"—I suddenly felt a thick finger jam directly into one side of my lower back—"he'll piss blood."

My eyes shot open, and I immediately wished that they hadn't. That gray-blue gaze was way too close, too intense. His finger lingered way too long, and there was a crackle in the air that had my senses on high alert.

Danger! Danger! Skinhead Boy is fucking touching you! He could kill you with that finger, BB! Kill you and eat your brains!

But those zombie eyes wouldn't let me move. Up close, they were so clear. Like two crystal balls that I wished would give me a glimpse into this twisted creature's soul. In my curious state of hypnosis, again, words tumbled unbidden from my mouth.

"Why'd you hit him?"

After a pause long enough to let me hope that maybe I hadn't actually asked my question out loud, he answered, "Because he called your little boyfriend a faggot."

About three million follow-up questions slammed into my throat at once:

> *A) Why would a Neo-Nazi looking motherfucker beat someone up that he doesn't even know for calling some other dude he doesn't know a faggot?*
>
> *B) Shouldn't he have given the kid a high five instead?*
>
> *C) Why would he call Lance my boyfriend? Lance is NOT my boyfriend. I mean, I want him to be my boyfriend. Jesus, I want to ride him like a pony*

> *everywhere I go and have all of his babies, but he's not my boyfriend.*
>
> *D) Why would anyone think Lance was gay in the first place? He's sooo dreamy.*

But the only thing I could squeak out was, "You were defending Lance?"

I never knew an eye roll could be so terrifying. *Shit.* I'd done it. I'd finally pissed him off with all my stupid fucking questions. Why did I always have to talk to the scary ones?

My mom still loved to tell people about the time I'd picked up my Happy Meal and sat down with a group of leather-clad bikers at McDonald's when I was three just so that I could ask the gnarliest-looking one why he had a ponytail. According to her, my exact words were, "Only girls are 'apposed to have ponytails."

My curiosity was going to get me straight murdered one day.

The skinhead, who now looked positively murderous himself, removed his hand from my back and placed it on my locker, just above my head. Cocking his head to the side again, he watched me, as if mulling over the best way to skin me alive, and of course, I just stood there, blinking up at him like a fucking dumbass.

Basic bodily functions like speaking, breathing, and running were completely out of my grasp. It was as if I'd been cornered by a coiled rattlesnake. A rattlesnake that just so happened to smell like dryer sheets, cigarettes, and a sweet hint of cologne.

"No," he said. "I was defending *you.*"

Too much. It was too intense. I broke eye contact and took a step backward, landing on the backpack I had forgotten was behind me and almost losing my balance. Turning around to pick it up, I took a deep breath and tried to regroup before facing him again. When I did, his ghostly eyes were crinkled at the corners, and his mouth was tipped up just slightly on one side. *Fucker.* He was actually enjoying watching me squirm.

Smirk still in place, he said, "When I was outside, I heard that little shit telling his buddy about the hard-on he had for 'the little redhead in the fishnets.' Couldn't argue with him there, Punk. I think you gave every guy in that parking lot a semi."

My face was suddenly on fire. *Oh God. I'm blushing! Is this really happening?*

He continued, but his smirk had been replaced by something that made my blood run cold. "When he saw that giant motherfucker's hands on you, he turned into a pissy little bitch." He spat the last word out through gritted teeth. "Told his buddy you must love taking it up the ass to be wasting your time with that queer."

Gulp. Breathe. What?

"S-so, so you punched him?"

The zombie-eyed skinhead leaned down toward my ear and didn't stop until I could feel his hot, venomous breath on my neck. "I. Beat. His. Fucking. Ass."

My limbs were moving on their own accord. Legs stumbling backward. Hands fumbling with backpack straps. "Um, thanks?" I mumbled, eyes darting everywhere but his. "I, uh, have to go … I'm gonna miss my … thanks again …"

"Knight," he announced as I turned and sprinted for the double doors. "Thanks, *Knight.*"

Fuck me.

Read the rest of BB and Knight's story at:
https://mybook.to/bbeastonskin

PLAYLIST

THIS PLAYLIST IS A collection of songs that I either mentioned in *Dying for Rain* or that I felt illustrated a feeling or a scene from the book. I am grateful to each and every one of the brilliant artists listed below. Their creativity fuels mine.

You can stream the playlist for free on Spotify: https://open.spotify.com/user/bbeaston

"Army of Me" by Björk
"Artist and Repertoire" by Envy on the Coast
"Bandito" by Twenty One Pilots
"Black Out Days" by Phantogram
"Champion" by Bishop Briggs
"Champion" by Fall Out Boy
"False God" by Taylor Swift
"Graveyard" by Halsey
"Hallelujah" by Paramore
"I Will Follow You into the Dark" by Death Cab for Cutie
"Jumpsuit" by Twenty One Pilots
"My Cell" by The Lumineers
"Neon Gravestones" by Twenty One Pilots
"Nightmare" by Halsey
"ocean eyes" by Billie Eilish

"Oh No!!!" by grandson
"Prison Sex" by TOOL
"Slip on the Moon" by DREAMCAR
"Start a Riot" by Duckwrth, Shaboozey
"Team" by Lorde
"The Ruler and the Killer" by Kid Cudi
"Weaker Girl" by BANKS
"you should see me in a crown" by Billie Eilish

Books by BB Easton

44 CHAPTERS ABOUT 4 MEN
Inspiration for the Netflix Original Series SEX/LIFE.

THE 44 CHAPTERS SPIN-OFF SERIES

Darkly funny. Deeply emotional. Shockingly sexy.
SKIN (Knight's backstory, Book 1)
SPEED (Harley's backstory, Book 2)
STAR (Hans's backstory, Book 3)
SUIT (Ken's backstory, Book 4)

THE RAIN TRILOGY

Intense, immersive, end-of-the-world romance.
PRAYING FOR RAIN
FIGHTING FOR RAIN
DYING FOR RAIN

GROUP THERAPY
Hilarious, heartwarming psychologist-client romcom.

DEVIL OF DUBLIN
A dark mafia romance steeped in Irish folklore.

ACKNOWLEDGMENTS

If you're reading this, that means you made it all the way to the end of The Rain Trilogy! Thank you so, so much for taking this journey with me. I've never written fiction before. My five previous books are all based on my real life, so this was a challenge of epic proportions. But if you've read *SUIT*, you know that I love nothing more than a good challenge. I learned so much during this process—mostly that writing fiction is hard as hell, but also that I have the best readers in the entire world. You guys show up. Whether I'm writing a sexy, comedic memoir; an angsty, semi-autobiographical New Adult series; or a gritty, dystopian romantic suspense trilogy, you guys are here for it. I love you for that.

I also love **Ken Easton**. I joke that I don't carry a purse; I carry a man. I bring Ken with me everywhere I go. He is the holder of my lipstick, the keeper of my schedule, the doer of my taxes, the mower of my lawn, and the hand on my elbow, preventing me from walking into traffic when I'm too busy talking to you all on social media to pay attention to my surroundings. He keeps me alive and fed and laughing and out of prison so that I can do what I love, and for that, we should *all* say, *Thank you.*

I'm also indebted to **my mom**, **Ken's mom**, and **Ken's sister** for watching my kids at the drop of a hat so that I can meet a deadline or catch a plane. It takes a village, y'all. Thank God I have a good one.

It also takes a village to edit these damn books. A huge, huge thank-you to my content editors, **Karla Nellenbach** and **Traci Finlay**; my copy editors, **Jovana Shirley** and **Ellie McLove**; my beta readers, **Sammie Lynn**, **Sara Snow**, and **Tracey Frazier**; and my proofreaders, **April C.**, **Michelle Beiger DePrima**, and **Rhonda Lind** for always, always squeezing me in when I need you, at least pretending to be excited about my books, and polishing them up quickly and thoroughly every single time. You guys are the first people I let read my work, and your sensitivity and enthusiasm are what give me the confidence to hit publish. I hope you know how much I appreciate you.

And as if editing them isn't hard enough, then I have to turn around and sell the damn things. Thank God I have the magical unicorns of **Bookcase Literary Agency—Flavia Viotti**, **Meire Dias**, and **Maria Napolitano**—and the rock stars of **Social Butterfly PR—Jenn Watson**, **Sarah Ferguson,** and **Brooke Nowiski**—on my team. Anytime I have good news to share, a book to publish, or a karaoke bar calling my name, you guys are always there with a thoroughly researched plan, a handful of Advil, and your Uber app on standby. Thank you for spreading the word about these stories and for getting them into as many new hands as possible. You are the wind beneath my wings.

And speaking of spreading the word, I couldn't do it without **all of my author friends**—especially you, **Colleen**, only because I haven't mentioned your name in this book yet. Thank you for selflessly sharing your platforms, your resources, your time, and your expertise to help me succeed. I've said it before, and I'll say it again. I don't have competitors; I have coworkers. I love you guys.

To **Larry Robins** and **J. Miles Dale**, thank you for believing in me. You took a quirky debut Frankenbook that was too sexy to be a comedic memoir and too autobiographical to be a romance novel and somehow turned it into a Netflix series. I don't know what the hell I did to deserve you, but I am eternally grateful to you both. I can't wait to squeeze you on the red carpet!

And as always, to the **readers, bloggers, and bookstagrammers of** #TeamBB, you guys are my ride-or-dies. Thank you for the gorgeous teasers, the comments and shares, the reviews that never fail to make me cry, the thoughtful gifts, and the relentless, rabid support you've showered me with over the years. You overwhelm me with your love, and I hope when you come see me at an event or interact with me online that you feel it returned tenfold. Also, all of your affection totally makes up for the fact that Ken is an emotional cyborg, so he thanks you, too. I yell at him a lot less now that I have you.

ABOUT THE AUTHOR

BB Easton is the *Wall Street Journal* bestselling author of *44 CHAPTERS ABOUT 4 MEN*, the hilarious, steamy, tell-all memoir that inspired the Netflix Original Series, *SEX/LIFE.* Within the first month, *SEX/LIFE* was viewed by 67 million households worldwide, making it the 3rd Most-Watched Netflix Original Series of all time.

BB was a stressed-out school psychologist and mother of two when the inspiration to write *44 CHAPTERS ABOUT 4 MEN* struck. Through that process, she rediscovered her passion for writing, became dangerously sleep-deprived, and finally mustered enough courage to quit her job and become a full-time author.

BB went on to publish four more wickedly funny, shockingly steamy, and heartwarmingly autobiographical books in the 44 CHAPTERS series: *SKIN*, *SPEED*, *STAR*, and *SUIT*. Since then, she's been hard at work writing fictional stories that appeal to her love for us-against-the-world romance, including a dystopian trilogy (*PRAYING FOR RAIN*), a psychologist-client romantic comedy (*GROUP THERAPY*), and a dark mafia romance (*DEVIL OF DUBLIN*).

You can find BB procrastinating in all of the following places:

Website: www.authorbbeaston.com

Instagram:
www.instagram.com/author.bb.easton

TikTok: https://vm.tiktok.com/ZMeEKRLyS/

Facebook: www.facebook.com/bbeaston

#TeamBB Facebook Group:
www.facebook.com/groups/BBEaston

Twitter: www.twitter.com/bb_easton

Pinterest: www.pinterest.com/artbyeaston

Goodreads: https://goo.gl/4hiwiR

BookBub:
https://www.bookbub.com/authors/bb-easton

Spotify:
https://open.spotify.com/user/bbeaston

Selling signed books, mugs, apparel, and original art on Etsy: www.etsy.com/shop/artbyeaston

And giving away free e-books from her bestselling author friends every month in her newsletter: www.artbyeaston.com/subscribe

CPSIA information can be obtained
at www.ICGtesting.com
Printed in the USA
LVHW100211051122
732386LV00003B/393

9 781732 700765